GRYMVEIL TALES

A Short Story Collection

Sianyn Leigh

CHAOS AND INK BOOKS, LLC

Published by Chaos and Ink Books, LLC

Quincy, IL 62301

www.ChaosInkBooks.com

First Paperback Edition: August 2024

Paperback edition ISBN: 978-1-964823-01-0

Electronic ISBN: 978-1-964823-00-3

Book Cover Designed by S. L. Black

Cover illustrations and interior elements by Tanarch, David Luu, Olya Creative Art, and Studio Gulden.

Dedicated to my partner, who offers endless support with zero nuance.

Special thanks to Kim Zieres for acting as soundboard, providing critique, and being my absolute bestie. You are invaluable as a friend and as a writing partner.
Extra special thanks to my editor, Robert Brown, for always knowing where the commas go.

CONTENTS

MY TURN

I never wanted to be a Fairy Godmother. It's not exactly a gig you choose. It's something you're born into, a genetic accident. Some people are born with brown eyes or blonde hair. I was born a Fairy Godmother.

It's not as glamorous as everyone makes it out to be. I'm always on call, apparating at the first plea for assistance from a physically blessed waif with a princess complex. It doesn't matter what I'm doing. I could be cooking lunch or in the shower and *poof!* I'm suddenly standing in all my glitter glory before an entitled miss ready to do her bidding. I have no control over my own life.

You might think it's wonderful to possess magic, granting wishes, pulling coaches and glass slippers from thin air. And it *is* great. For the heroine. But I can't use any of that magic on myself.

Being a Fairy Godmother is a curse. You spend your whole life pleasing other people, giving everyone else their happy ending. What do I get for myself? A lifetime of servitude to foolish whims and vain requests. I can't even bippity-bop the frizz from my hair.

As if that wasn't enough, my life sentence lasts a lot longer than any average Joe could expect to suffer. Fairy Godmothers are notoriously long-lived. Now, I'm not talking still spry at ninety-nine. I mean, still popping out of nowhere to fulfill wishes at the relatively young age of five hundred. I've got a few centuries to go before my retirement plan kicks in, a generous 401—*dissolve into mist and blow away on the breeze*—k.

I am a normal person. I put my gossamer bloomers on one foot at a time. I have feelings, hobbies, ambitions. When I was a wee elf, I wanted to be a professional pearl diver. Unfortunately, I learned fairy wings don't do well underwater. As I grew up, I wanted to have a career, a husband, 2.5 kids and a dog. To be wooed into domestic bliss. I wanted the same dream all my clients wanted. But the closest I'll ever get to a romantic evening is keeping Prince Charming's hands to himself until he's officially said "I do."

Maybe that's why it happened. A person can only take so many broken dreams and repressed desires before they finally snap. And snap I did.

***

The sun rose on a morning much like any other. I was pulled from my slumber to attend yet another whining session over how some useless ninny's perfect life could get just a little more perfect.

"Please, Fairy Godmothers, bless my daughter with your wondrous gifts."

Rubbing bleary eyes, I shook the sleep from my body and took in my surroundings. I was in the audience hall of a castle, next to two other Fairy Godmothers I knew from our annual Godmother Picnic and Scavenger Hunt.

Before us were the figures of a king and queen. You know the type: wealthy, attractive, admired by all, never had a rough day in their life. Their darling of a princess lay between them, a newborn bundle of joy swaddled in silk and rocked in an ivory cradle. Shiny blonde hair, twinkling blue eyes, a sweet nature and a kind heart.

Her loving parents would see she lacked for nothing and betroth her to the most handsome of princes when the time came. She was exactly the kind of perfect, privileged, *doesn't need my help* kind of person I was always being commanded to improve.

"Oh, look at the sweet baby. Babies are so adorable."

Buttercup leaned over the cradle to make cutesy noises at the infant, wings fluttering in excitement.

The matronly Blue clasped her hands deferentially before her, all but groveling on the ground.

"Monarchs such as yourself could not deserve a more perfect child."

I rolled my eyes. The others were always so simpering towards their clients, glad of the opportunity to heap unwarranted blessings upon the already blessed.

Buttercup glared at me and Blue gave me a sharp nudge when I failed to sing praises immediately.

"Yeah, she's real cute," I mumbled.

Of course, she was cute! Her parents were the genetic cream of the crop and whatever nature hadn't bestowed on her, mommy and daddy could more than afford to buy. Looks, friends, status; this chick had it all, and she couldn't even walk yet.

"We would be honored if you would give her your blessings," the Queen crooned, lowering her head slightly in feigned respect.

No one really respected Fairy Godmothers. Why should they? We didn't choose whom to bless and whom not to. We were compelled to grant the wishes of any heroine or hero who asked. The powers that be put the system in place long ago to keep things predictable. No upsetting the status quo in fairy tales!

Blue dropped into a deep curtsy. "The honor is entirely ours."

She removed her wand from her sleeve with a flourish, brandished it over the cooing infant and cleared her throat.

"I gift you, dear Princess, with beauty such as none possess. Your eyes like bluebells, your hair like silk! None shall match you in grace and ilk."

She wiggled her wand over the infant's face and a tiny shower of light sprinkled from the tip. With a smile and a nod towards the royal couple, Blue shuffled back into line alongside me.

Buttercup stepped forward for her turn. She tapped her wand against her palm briskly, sending little sparks flying. The infant laughed at the minute fireworks, smiling with perfect rose petal lips. Magic primed, Buttercup drew up her shoulders and took in a breath.

"Beauty and grace is well and fine, but beauty in song is more divine. I give to you the gift of voice so melodious and true, it will cheer the bluest of blue."

Buttercup applauded herself while the King and Queen smirked at each other. With these gifts, they could secure any prince in the entire world to be their daughter's husband. It made me sick. This princess hadn't needed any extra talent or beauty. The kingdom her parents presided over was wealthy and secure enough to attract a suitable prince without irresistible charms. There were plenty of other, less privileged girls who would benefit from fairy blessings much more than this child. But that isn't how the story goes.

And now it was my turn to bestow more gifts.

I stepped forward and gave a great wracking cough, delaying for time to think of an appropriate spell. What could I possibly gift her with that she didn't already possess? Unmatched cooking skills? An affinity with animals? Being able to weave straw into gold was a little overkill in my opinion.

I was saved from having to speak by a sudden plume of smoke and a deafening pop as a witch with dark robes and darker eyes appeared in the center of the room. The queen screamed and the king called for his guards, but all the witch had to do was make a sweeping gesture with her staff to keep them all at bay.

Envy rolled over me. This woman commanded her power. Used it for herself, and no one else. How I burned to cast for my own ends.

"You did not invite me, oh great liege, to this gift-giving party?" The witch sounded more pleased than offended. Her smile twisted into a snarl. "I am crushed. Crushed as I was on the night you forsook me for your lovely wife."

Witches are jealous creatures. Resentful of the beauty denied them, of the love denied them. Steeped in envy for all the things they could never have in a normal life, all the things I and my kind gave heroines as a matter of course. It was what separated Fairy Godmothers from Evil Witches. Godmothers were born; Witches were made.

"Then, allow me now to bestow a gift upon the lovely creature."

The witch stepped closer to the cradle. Buttercup and Blue took a fearful step back, but I stood my ground. A witch had no cause to hurt me. My life was not worthy of envy.

The king reached a staying hand for her black-clad arm, but dared not touch her.

"Please, I beg of you, leave this place and never return. We do not desire your gifts."

Anger flared over the witch as a visible indigo flame. The effect was impressive, if mostly cosmetic.

"I did not ask your permission!"

Turning back to the cradle, she lifted her staff and began, "Loved by all you meet, in beauty and song you shall indeed excel. But before midnight on your eighteenth year, a finger shall you prick on the needle of a spinning wheel and your last breath *expel*."

In a blinding flash and a cloud of sulfur, the witch disappeared. Fairly standard as curses went.

A wave of gasps swept the room from the shocked onlookers as the smoke dissipated. The queen collapsed to the floor in a heap of tears and wails. The king stood, head bobbing in indecision as he visibly struggled to determine whether he should comfort his wife or coddle his daughter. Finally, he turned to me.

"Please, Godmother, save my daughter from this evil curse," he pleaded.

"Make it so she only sleeps, not dies," Blue suggested.

"And a handsome prince will come wake her with a kiss," Buttercup added.

I thought about it, I truly did. I could make another happy ending.

But I was tired of happy endings.

I was tired of making everyone's dreams come true but my own. Where was my devastating beauty, my unsurpassed talent? Why did I never get the knight in shining armor? It was always about someone else, and I'd had enough. I couldn't take it anymore.

No, that's not right. I *wouldn't* take it anymore. This time, I was going to do something for myself. With malicious intent in my heart and a wave of my wand, I spoke my generous gift.

"I cannot stop the witch's curse said and done, but you can't prick your finger if you have none."

Buttercup and Blue choked on a gasp as the princess' perfectly formed hands disappeared, her tiny wrists ending in a smooth stump. I smiled as the queen wailed and the king shouted condemnation, but once bestowed, a fairy's blessing cannot be taken back. We're only allowed one gift per client. As Buttercup and Blue had already spent their blessings, they could do nothing to override mine.

Pride filled me as I gestured at the now fingerless child.

"I have saved the princess. The curse cannot be fulfilled. She will keep her beauty and her song, and will never prick her finger on a spinning wheel. I have done as you asked."

Falling to his knees, the king openly wept over his altered daughter.

"That's not what I meant," he sobbed.

I sneered down at him, disgusted at his display. He should show more gratitude for my life-saving efforts. A rich, talented, adored princess bearing a Witch's Curse could do a lot worse than some missing hands. Besides, it would give her some perspective on her place in life.

"A challenge will do her good. Builds character. She'll have it easy enough, anyway."

I gave my wand a hard swipe, willing it into a slender, twisted staff. Tapping the end on the ground, my pink gossamer bloomers shifted into a long dress of deep blue velvet as my wings shriveled and shrunk into my skin. Shaking my hair loose from its bun, it grew until it reached my waist in wild tendrils that swayed in the air currents like flames upon the wind. My transformation felt like the falling away of shackles.

I was free.

Buttercup trembled before me as Blue stuttered, "Shimmer, how could you?"

"Call me Shiver. Now, if you'll excuse me, I'm going to pay a visit to the Swan Princess. I'll show her how a goose gets dressed for dinner."

I flexed my fingers into a fist, feeling the magic gather at my will and my will alone. Power surged through me, ready to fulfill whatever destiny I desired. My smile widened. I took one last look at the distraught court and, with a twist of my hand, poofed several miles from the castle in an explosion of midnight mist. A feeling of unfettered joy swelled my heart.

It's my turn now.

QUACKERS AND MILK

Everyone knew the abandoned house on Cherry Wood Lane was haunted. And I mean KNEW knew. It wasn't a rumor. There were photos, videos, and a whole webpage devoted to sightings. It was once featured on an episode of some ghost hunting show. An exorcist even tried to cleanse it once, putting on a big dog and pony show for the local TV crew.

But the ghost was back the very next night, waving at folks from the window like he had something important to say. Nothing ever came out but groaning awful enough to make you want to stab your ears closed. The ghost hunters called him The Moaning Man, but I just called him Steve. Not out loud, of course, just in my head when I thought about him. *There's poor Steve, at it again.*

I had a lot of time on my hands and not many friends, so researching the town's famous ghost seemed like a good use of my evenings. It wasn't hard to uncover The Moaning Man's history.

It was boring, really, as much as it was tragic. Steve Mannon: accountant; married with three kids; lived in an old Victorian house in the historic neighborhood of town. Tripped down the basement stairs one day and died. The haunting began immediately after, and the poor widow grabbed the kids and ran as far away as she could get. A few others tried to live there over the years, but no one ever stayed long. 40 years later, old Steve was still walking around the place, moaning at anyone who got close enough to hear him.

Sneaking into the place for a closer peek or even a quick photo had become a rite of passage among the local kids. You had to spend the night in Steve's old bedroom or you couldn't be part of the cool kids. Anyone who chickened out would forever be branded a coward, even after graduation.

As the new kid in town, I was desperate to make a couple friends, even if that meant disturbing the dead. That's how I found myself staring up at the window from across the street Friday evening. I didn't care whether I was part of the "cool kids" or not, but Erica was in the cool kids, and she was one of the few people who seemed interested in my company. So, when Ben found out I had yet to complete that particular initiation, we all made the trek down to the famed house.

"You ever seen The Moaning Man, Jacey?" Ben asked, looking at me with that half smirk, half sneer that made me want to slap the skin right off his face. He didn't like me—the feeling was mutual—but he let me hang around because I was Erica's friend.

I shrugged, turning away so my face wouldn't give away how much I disliked him. "Just on, like, memes and stuff. Saw an episode of Grave Adventures about it."

And on The Moaning Man website, the Ghostipedia page, and the newspaper clippings from the library archive. But I wasn't about to tell him that and risk looking like some kind of ghost stalker.

"Well, then, you're in for a treat, newbie. Get your butt up there and say hi," Ben drawled, followed by a scattering of snickers from the rest of our group.

I shifted my weight from foot to foot, frowning so hard my face muscles strained. Reading about Steve and watching internet videos was one thing, but I knew well enough than to go poking at ghosts in real life. On my own. In an abandoned building that probably was in desperate need of some repairs. I wasn't too keen on having to stay the night, either. What if it got cold and froze to death? What if I had to pee? I doubt the plumbing still worked.

The silence stretched a little too long as they waited for me to take up the challenge and Ben wasn't about to let my hesitation slide.

"What? Don't you have the balls?" He snickered and the other boys laughed with him. Ben smirked at me over Erica's head, silently challenging me to ignore the jibe. And I fully intended to ignore him. His lame attempt to bait me wasn't the least bit impressive.

"It doesn't take balls to be an idiot," Erica snapped, eliciting a giggle from Rachelle, and Ben's face flamed bright at the implication. She turned to me, laying her fingertips on my arm, looking at me with genuine concern and sympathy.

"You don't have to play their stupid games," she assured me. "You don't have anything to prove."

Well, I *hadn't* had anything to prove until that moment. Her well-meaning sympathy jabbed at my sense of pride and I suddenly very much wanted to prove I didn't need her protection from Ben and his cronies. I wasn't afraid, not of Ben's opinions and not of old Moaning Man Steve, who couldn't figure out he was dead and needed to cross over—or whatever it was spirits were supposed to do. It didn't stop the shiver that went down my spine when I glanced up at the house or the chill that balled in the pit of my stomach, but I couldn't back out.

"No, no, I got it," I said, managing to voice a confidence I absolutely did not feel. "Piece of cake."

I adjusted the backpack on my shoulder—filled with a few essentials like snacks and water to last the night, a battery-powered lantern, an old worn copy of a Neil Gaiman book—and tossed Erica a reassuring smile.

"I'll catch you in the morning," I promised, turning to cross the street.

"Make sure you send me a picture every hour to prove you're there!" Ben called. "No pictures, no proof!"

I waved my hand over my head in acknowledgement of the command as I trotted across the street. More than one kid had tried to beat the system by sneaking out the back door for more comfortable quarters while swearing they'd braved it out the whole night, only to be found out as a cheat later by some neighborhood snitch. I had no intention of trying to pull any tricks and risk even worse teasing than I already suffered.

I stepped past the rotted and leaning front gate, the weeds stretching across the walkway scratching at my ankles as I passed. The boards of the sagging porch creaked loudly as I stepped up and I halted immediately. I took a half-step back, wondering if I should try another way in. Falling through the warped and pitted porch before I even got inside didn't sound like a great start to the challenge.

"Keep going," Ben hollered, followed by a string of unrepeatable insults.

Taking a deep breath and steeling myself for the probable fall, I stepped onto the porch again, pushing at the cracked and peeling front door. The hinges squealed, but it swung open easily enough. It was impossible to keep a house with such a reputation locked and after about the fiftieth break-in, the property manager had given up and just stopped replacing the lock.

The setting sun filtered through what was left of the curtains, illuminating the foyer just enough to move around without fumbling. The inside had once been a late Victorian with vibrant wallpaper and polished floors, still boasting the original woodwork. But decades of sitting vacant and hosting illicit teen parties had left the walls faded and torn, marker and spray paint spread across the surface. The wood had begun to crack, splintering around corners and weak spots, and the window frames showed signs of water damage from rain seeping through warped frames.

In the living room just off the foyer, empty bottles and stray snack wrappers littered the floor, with a couple of ratty, obviously salvaged cushions as makeshift seats. I wandered through the rest of the downstairs—the kitchen, dining room, study—finding all of them in similar condition. I made my way for the stairs, surprised the treads didn't creak more, though the handrail was a bit wobbly.

The front bedroom was Steve's room—well, the master bedroom, anyway. I moved to the window—Steve's Window—and took out my phone for my first picture proof for Ben. I angled the phone so I could get my face, the room, and a bit of the window in the same shot and waited for the flash. It wasn't until I sent it to the group chat that I noticed something in the corner of the picture, just over my shoulder. I enlarged the pic and squinted, just making out the blurred image of what appeared to be the face of someone standing right behind me.

The phone slipped from my hand as my body went cold and I spun around with what I can only embarrassingly call a squeak.

Yep, there he was, ol' Steve himself, just standing behind me like he wasn't a full-on apparition forty years past his death date. I can't say I was pleased to see him. I liked the idea of ghosts; I wasn't too keen on actually meeting them. He wasn't a pretty sight either, even if he was mostly opaque.

Ghosts tend to look the way they died, and Steve's untimely demise had come from a long drop down some steep stairs. His left arm hung at an awkward angle, swinging like a branch in the breeze. A bone protruded out from his khaki-clad leg, accentuated by the dark stain spreading around it. But what really got to me was his face.

The upper-left temple had a caved-in look, the eyeball bulging out like one of those stress balls. The left cheek had been split from the corner of the mouth to his cheekbone and the jaw snapped at the hinge, leaving his lower mandible in a lopsided dangle that exposed much more of the inner workings of a mouth than I wanted privy to. It looked like he had bounced off every step on his fatal fall, and it had not been graceful.

I wanted to look away from the gruesome sight, but terrified if I did, he'd lunge at me or something. I don't know if ghosts can actually attack people or not—the shows and websites never seem to agree—but I wasn't about to test the theory myself. I bent down, reaching one arm out to fumble for my phone while keeping my eyes glued to the specter.

Steve seemed to realize I was aware of him because he began moaning at me, jaw flapping from one hinge as he slowly reached his right arm towards me. I tried to scramble back, not willing to risk a ghost-touch, but scrambling while crouched isn't easy. I fell hard on my rump instead, crab-crawling several feet away.

Steve didn't follow. He stayed where he was, arm still out, the incessant moaning gurgling from his broken face. The impulse to grab my phone and run tensed every muscle in my body, but I forced myself to stay on the floor. Everyone ran from Steve. Despite half the school boasting they'd braved a night in the house, the truth was very few of them ever stayed long after Steve made an appearance. I couldn't blame them. Anyone who saw something like this coming at them in the middle of the night would run.

Only I wasn't running. I couldn't let Ben be right. I had to prove to everyone I could cut it; I wasn't a loser. And I didn't want to disappoint Erica, either. I mean, she said she didn't care, but not caring if I chickened out and being really impressed I hadn't were two very different things. Given the choice, I wanted to impress her.

After a few more incredibly tense minutes of just sitting there and Steve just moaning at me, I began to relax. Yeah, he was scary-looking, but he wasn't threatening. He just sorta stood there, flapping his jaw and waving his hand. That's when I started to pick up the cadence in his moans. It wasn't just gurgle after gurgle. There was a pattern to it, a rising and falling, some moans short, others longer, with different pitches and lilts. Words. He was trying to say words.

"Hey, dude, I can't understand what you're saying." Steve paused, cocking his head at me slightly. I pointed towards his face. "It's your jaw, man. I can't make out the words with your jaw all jacked up."

Steve straightened, looking at me with his one good eye like I'd somehow insulted him. Raising his good arm, he felt at his face, the left eye bulging even more as he seemed to discover his dislocated jaw for the first time in nearly half a century. He pushed up on the broken side, trying to fit the hinge back together, but it just dropped again as soon as he let go.

He stared at me, eliciting a groan that almost sounded like a question. I stared back and shrugged. Steve sighed, shoulders sagging, and bowed his head in defeat. I looked down, too, suddenly ashamed I had made a ghost feel bad. Then, with a grunt, Steve reached down and unthreaded a shoelace with one hand.

I watched in disgusted awe as he held one end of the shoelace between the roof of his mouth and his tongue, while tying a loop in the other end with his fingers. He worked the straight end between the flesh and the jawbone, threaded it through the loop, wrapped it over the top of his head, pulling it tight and tying it around itself under his chin. As he pulled up all the slack, the looped end raised his jaw into something close to where it was supposed to be. The bones would never fit back together right, but the shoelace now kept the lower mandible from swinging around.

Steve spoke a couple of practice words, literally *one-two, one-two*, testing his new speech capabilities with his jaw raised up at the proper height. The air whistled through the gap in his cheek and his tongue kept slipping out the side, but they were intelligible now.

Taking a deep breath and pinning me with a firm glare, Steve said, "It's not where you go, it's what you do."

Whatever I was expecting Steve to say, it wasn't that. *Get out*, *beware*, a good old-fashioned *boo*, even. But stale life advice? You never heard that on any of the ghost-hunting shows or true haunting biographies.

"Talk about ideas, not people," he continued.

"Uh, yeah, okay."

"Nothing good ever happens after midnight."

Hideous appearance and incessant moaning aside, Steve was quickly turning into the least scary haunting I had ever heard about. Relief loosened my tense muscles as I realized staying the entire night here wasn't going to be much of a challenge at all, provided I could stay awake through all the tired old dad advice.

I put my hand up to halt the flow of words. "Okay, Steve, I'm gonna stop you there. Is this, like, your whole haunting schtick? Just dropping advice on unwary visitors? Cuz it's a little weird, man."

Steve drew in a breath as if to say more, then paused. His brow furrowed, and he glanced away as if he'd find the answer scrawled in marker on the wall. Then, with a groan, he bent his good leg until he was sitting on the floor, heaving a sigh heavy with defeat. When he turned to look at me again, his right eye was filled with such raw emotion, I felt a stab of guilt for hurting his feelings again.

I sank down to the floor with him, crossing my legs under me and resting my elbows on my knees.

"I'm sorry, I just thought you'd be scarier, you know. Like, try to chase me away or something."

"I died before I could finish being a dad," Steve said, drawing in a breath after every third word like it took effort to get it all out. "I wanted to tell my kids so much, to be there for them. I missed so much, and they moved so far away before I could tell them everything. Now, I can't cross over."

"Cross over? Oh, so like, sharing all your advice is like your unfinished business?"

That I had heard of before. Every Medium from podcasts to blogs talked about helping souls complete unfinished business so they could *go into the light*, or whatever. Usually, it was something dramatic like solving their murder or revealing where they hid treasure. But Steve hadn't been a murder victim or a famous pirate or any of that.

He'd just been an average middle-class dad in the Midwest. Figured his unfinished business would be equally as boring. He was probably more than ready to cross over by now, after 40 years alone in a rotting house. The only thing I knew about religion was that song by R.E.M., but whatever waited on the other side had to be better than just floating around moaning at people. I was stuck there for the night, but Steve would be stuck there for eternity if he couldn't cross over. Maybe I could help with that. Not like there was anything else to do for the next 8 hours.

"Well, you could tell me everything you wanted to tell your kids," I offered, shrugging. "I don't know if it qualifies as finishing your business, but I'm willing to help you try."

Tears welled in Steve's good eye as what remained of his lips tried to stretch into a smile. His other eye just bulged out more, leaking a viscous-looking dark fluid I didn't want to think about. At least ghosts didn't have a smell. Otherwise, I might have changed my mind right then.

"You would do that for me?" Steve ask-moaned, the words catching as emotion swelled his throat.

I shrugged again, shifting uncomfortably at the display of gratitude. "Sure, why not? I never had a dad to give me advice, and you never got a chance to share all yours with your kids. We could consider it an even trade."

Smiling, Steve pulled himself to his feet once more, cleared his throat and took a deep breath. As he started listing off all the tidbits of wisdom he had learned over his life, I scooted over to the dingy mattress. It wasn't the best, but if I was going to be sitting for the next several hours, it felt worlds better on my rear than the hardwood floor. Back against the wall, munching on a bag of chips from my snack stash, I paid attention as best I could while Steve rambled on.

Enjoy the little moments. Find what makes you happy and get paid for it. Always be true to yourself. Never spend more than you make. He emphasized each bit of droll advice with a personal life story, laboriously groaned out with such strain I feared the shoelace holding up his jaw would break. But maybe ghost laces didn't break or speaking wasn't as much effort as it seemed, because that knot held through long explanations of how taxes work, to the importance of budgeting, to how to shop for a mortgage.

Every hour, Steve paused so I could take another selfie for Ben. I even got Steve in a couple of shots, though his grey opaque figure was barely visible in the background. Finally, just as the first birds began to wake up and chirp with the dawn, Steve seemed to run out of sage life hacks, his words trickling away to silence.

"Thanks, Steve," I said when he didn't speak again. "That was great. Very helpful. I should probably remember some of it."

I wouldn't, but I should. Part of me wished I had recorded that bit about taxes. It was likely better than anything I was going to hear from my economics teacher.

"Do you have anything left to share? It's almost time for me to get out of here."

"What has four wheels and flies?" he asked, one side of his mouth pulled up in a smirk as his good eye watched me expectantly. "A garbage truck."

I groaned and rolled my eyes. I should have known this was coming. What always follows Dad Advice but Dad Jokes?

"Why did the cookie go to the doctor? It was feeling crumby," Steve continued, chuckling at his own punchline in a rusty wheeze. I smiled, not at the joke—that was bad— but at how happy telling it made him.

"I have a joke about pizza, but it's too cheesy."

The wheezing intensified, sounding painfully close to what you'd get if you scraped a bunch of rusty metal together. The pun was even more painful to hear. Unable to take a second more of his cheesy jokes,

I pushed off the old mattress and grabbed my backpack, slipping my phone back in my pocket. Now that the sun was lifting over the horizon, I didn't need the ambient glow of my lock screen to see.

"Okay, Steve, I gotta go. It's been swell, but the swelling's gone down," I quipped, earning another rusty chuckle. "I really hope you can find closure or whatever and cross over. Peace out."

I extended my right hand for a fist bump. After a brief hesitation, Steve did the same, his curled fingers passing right through my own, but I suppose it's the thought that counts.

I nodded a final farewell and turned for the door. Steve made a grunting moan and I turned one more time to see what he wanted.

"What do you call two ducks and a cow?" His smile was different now, the jovial lines smoothed into one of peace and acceptance. As the sunlight streamed through the window, beaming right into Steve and onto the hardwood below, he faded even more. Then more, until he was barely visible at all.

"Quackers and milk."

With that final whisper, Steve was gone into whatever afterlife awaited beyond. I glanced around the room, empty now but for debris and dust, and chuckled. He'd done it. He'd finally finished his business, free to cross over. And helping Steve finish his goal had helped me finish mine. I was one of the cool kids now, even if I now knew more about taxes and corporate office culture than I ever wanted to know.

GRYM DASH

It was hard to make ends meet as a Witch these days. It seemed everyone from weekend oracles to big box stores was hopping onto the Magic for Sale train, driving prices to rock-bottom levels. Independent Witches like Jaslene couldn't compete, forced to price services so low it barely covered the cost of spell components just to keep your name in the game. Most had full-time jobs in non-magical fields to pay the bills, reduced to practicing spellcraft as a side hustle, pushed out of their traditional family business by mass market spell-slingers who could produce cheap, temporary enchantments at half the price of a solitary practitioner.

So, when Jaslene had seen the flyer looking for participants in a magical creatures only race with a big prize for the winner, she'd been more than a little intrigued. According to the website, there were no restrictions on the breed of the mount as long as they were from the Grym (the magical dimension that bled into the mortal world with frightening regularity), and the rider didn't use any magical enhancements to improve performance. Jaslene's familiar Sweetie had never competed in anything before, but the five thousand dollar prize money was too good to pass up, especially with the Past Due notices accumulating quickly. Desperate for cash to keep her artisanal enchantments business afloat, she'd registered her devoted Hellhound for the race, throwing caution to the wind and her pointed hat into the ring.

Now, lined up with the other contestants, Jaslene wasn't so confident. Hellhounds were fast, sure, and effective personal bodyguards for the average City Witch. But Sweetie was a house familiar, a personal companion. She wasn't trained to stand against larger, more aggressive, more *mythical* creatures than the average drunken creep on a late-night walk home. And while combat was expressly forbidden in the race's rules, Jaslene couldn't help but feel nervous when she'd noticed Sweetie was practically mundane next to the other racers.

A wyvern four contestants down let out another piercing squeal and Jaslene dug her fingers deeper into the thick black fur of Sweetie's coat, seeking comfort in her soft warmth. The giant dog turned to give her a reassuring prod with her nose, feeling the Witch's unease through their bond. The sound of stamping feet and impatient huffs filled the air, adding to her tension and Jaslene was grateful for her familiar's protective presence. A flash of brown caught the corner of her eye, and she looked down to see a pink and green fairy riding a long-legged hare. The fairy's gossamer wings sparkled in the sun as the large hare fidgeted in place.

The fairy smiled up at her in greeting. "Hi! I'm Pye, and this is Pudden. This is gonna be loads of fun, isn't it?"

Jaslene raised her eyebrows, taking in the sight of the tiny fairy and her anxious mount. "Is that a rabbit? Like, just a regular rabbit?"

Pye giggled, the sound tinkling like broken glass. "Oh, no, silly! This is a Marche Hare. It can walk on anything. Water; air; even your dreams!"

Jaslene didn't doubt the fairy's claims—she was no expert in Veil creatures—but she did doubt the safety of such a small animal, especially when the centaur's hoof came within centimeters of crushing its skull.

"Hey, watch it, buddy," Jaslene snapped, pinning the human half with an angry glare. "No maiming the other contestants. It's in the rules."

The centaur peered down his nose at her, letting his eyes roam in a way that made her skin crawl before tossing back his model-worthy hair. "Sorry, sweetheart, but when you're this big, you don't notice little things."

He flexed as he said it, twisting his upper body to give her the best view of his rippling biceps and clenching his haunches to make the smooth hide ripple over taut muscles. Great, he was the centaur version of a Gym Bro.

"Unbelievable," Jaslene muttered, lips curling into a sneer at the uncouth display. Next to her, the fairy let out a string of colorful insults that would make even the most seasoned troll blush. The centaur didn't seem to hear any of it. His dismissive attitude and superior air raised Jaslene's hackles high.

"So, how are *you* here?" she demanded, gesturing vaguely at the track around them. The rules clearly stated each rider had to have a magical creature to race. It didn't say anything about magical creatures registering by themselves. Did a centaur count as a creature or a person? "Don't you have to have something to ride?"

The centaur smiled lasciviously and wiggled his eyebrows at her. "I will if you play your cards right."

Jaslene rolled her eyes at his tasteless come-on and the fairy let loose another barrage of inventive phrases.

"The Witch has a point," the High Fae on the centaur's other side interjected, his large, stone-skinned gargoyle looming behind him. "I mean, you can't very well be your own mount, can you? Is that even legal?"

"Are you asking him if he's man or horse?" the sorcerer perched atop a writhing basilisk snorted. "You Fae are so classist."

That comment got a rise out of the unicorn rider, and pretty soon the whole line erupted into a cacophony of raised voices, each clamoring for their interpretation of the rules to be heard over the others, several calling for the centaur to be disqualified. As tensions rose, the animals became more agitated, snapping and stomping with greater frequency. Jaslene leaned into Sweetie, thankful their place on the starting line was at the far end—plenty of room for a hasty retreat if all-out battle broke out. The Hellhound, alerted by her Witch's unease, kept a wary eye on the others but remained outwardly calm.

"Hey, hey, hey! Settle down!" The officiate stepped over the track line, voice booming through a bullhorn as she called the line to order. "I already went over this with the judges. There's nothing in the rules that says the creature and the rider can't be the same beast. He will not be disqualified for being his own rider. Or, own mount. Whatever."

The centaur gave a mock bow, tossing a smug smile at his would-be ousters. Some riders grumbled, but no further challenges were raised. An electronic bell rang across the track eight times, signaling to the waiting crowd the race was about to begin. The officiate turned towards the stands and Jaslene took in a deep, bracing breath. She forced her fingers to unclench in Sweetie's fur, willing her muscles to relax and her nerves to unfrazzle. She had no chance of even coming close to winning if she couldn't keep calm. Sweetie swung her head around to give her a supportive boop with her nose and Jaslene's tensions eased further.

"Welcome to the first annual Grym Dash!"

The crowd cheered as the riders raised their hands in greeting. The officiate waved one arm in a hushing motion and the clamor died as quickly as it had risen.

"May I present to you our impressive lineup of competitors: Renowned Veil trainer Bob Taylor, riding Kay Mera, the chimera of O'Flannagan's Extravaganza Circus!"

The Circus was famous in the region for having exclusively Veil creatures, so Bob and his mount were considered local celebrities of a sort and the crowd cheered accordingly. The chimera's triple heads tossed and turned, excited by the noise of the crowd. The lion head roared while the goat head protruding from its back screamed in protest against the snake head whipping around to hiss in its ears. Bob, holding on to the goat horns as reins, jerked the head sharply, eliciting a plaintive bleat before all three heads fell silent and watchful.

"Next, on the gryphon, Sunny, we have equestrian trained Sara O'Malley,"—the gryphon dropped into a low bow, golden wings spread forward to touch the ground at his front paws—"followed by Aos Si Ward Master Blythe Gwinny and the unicorn Cob-lee-det, uh, Cob-len-lad-ety, no, uh, -"

"Coblynlladdtywysogionenfys!"

"And the unicorn, Colby!"

The willowy-thin Fae maiden nudged the purple-dappled unicorn onto his hind legs. He raised his gold-tipped horn high in the air, mane shimmering white and gold like it was coated in glitter. Jaslene shivered, glad several riders stood between her and the fabled beast. Unicorns were beautiful, but those horns were made for stabbing and they often had an attitude to match.

"Thorn Berry the Brownie, riding the peryton, Fleetstreet."

The brownie, in his tailored brown and green riding uniform, waved from atop the sleek, winged deer to little applause except for a very enthusiastic gaggle of brownies at the top of the bleachers.

"And I have a very special treat for you today. Competing together in the same event for the very first time, the Sorcerer Alistair Crowhand on the basilisk Soul Crusher, and his famed rival, magician David Nichols and his wyvern End Game!"

The crowd erupted into a roar of excitement as the two riders allowed their mounts to step forward to pose for the fans. The basilisk, a triple-leather mask strapped over her eyes, undulated under her master's commanding hand, long forked tongue lashing in and out like a red whip. The wyvern put on a similar display, fanning his neck frill and stretching out his winged legs in an impressive stretch. Jaslene knew the wyvern was little more than a trained performer, all flash and little bite—though the same could not be said of his unpredictable rider. The magician was known to throw a curse over light insults and wasn't above engaging in a magic-soaked brawl. The Sorcerer had a somewhat more sinister reputation around town, but how much was bluster and how much earned, she didn't know.

The officiate waved her arm for silence again and the crowd reluctantly settled down as the star competitors stepped back into their places.

"Let's hear you give that warm of a welcome to Aos Si and Professor of Fae History at the Veil Technical Institute, Jaron Birch and his gargoyle companion, Basalt!"

The round of applause for the elegant Fae and his hulking gargoyle seemed paltry in comparison to what his fellow racers had received, more polite than enthused. The Aos Si lord crossed his arms in a pout of disappointment and glared at his companion as if hoping he could do something to ignite the crowd, but the gargoyle only shrugged.

"You may have seen our eighth competitor in the latest Este Lauder campaign, centaur model Anerides Kekasmos Eudaimon the 3rd!"

The centaur strutted in place, twisting his upper body in the classic Archer Pose, one arm outstretched while the other bent as if holding a bow. A few muscle-hungry girls in the bleachers squealed, but otherwise Jaslene was pleased to hear the applause lacked the gusto of previous introductions.

"And the Marche Hare ridden by a sparkly sprite, Pudden and Pye."

Pye urged Pudden out onto the track several feet until they were in view of the crowd. There was more intrigued interest than clapping, and Jaslene could well imagine the bets being placed on such a minuscule rider's chances against the giant beasts that filled the track. Mundane hares were fast and agile and it was logical to assume a magical one would be even more so. But could a hare, even one who could run on anything, outpace a speeding basilisk or a galloping peryton?

"And finally, we have Solitary Witch Jaslene Sharpe and her Hellhound familiar, Sweetie!"

Jaslene wasn't a pseudo-celebrity, brand ambassador, or particularly novel-looking, so she wasn't surprised by the cursory, almost reluctant clapping she received from the crowd. But she did want to show off a little, just to let the spectators know she wasn't a complete underdog.

"Come on, show them what you're made of," Jaslene urged, leaning close to whisper in her familiar's ear. "Just a little flame, so they know you've got Brimstone in your soul."

Still distracted by the feel of her companion's unease and the restless shuffling of the larger creatures, Sweetie only managed to puff her coat out, eyes taking on the barest glimmer of a fiery glow and she let out a half-hearted snort, a few thin tendrils of smoke curling up from her flaring nostrils.

A couple of less-than-polite jeers made a flush rise up Jaslene's cheeks and Sweetie whimpered, nudging at the Witch's arm to apologize for her poor performance. She gave the fluffy hound a reassuring pat and swung her leg over Sweetie's back to settle herself into position. Let the crowd underestimate them; it would make it that much more impressive when they saw just how quickly a Hellhound could move when they needed to.

The officiate turned towards the row of racers and the tension along Jaslene's shoulders rose. In just a few minutes, she'd either be taking a check to the bank, or limping home to a mound of bills with no hope of reviving her business. Taking another steadying breath, she let it out slowly and blocked everything from her mind but this exact moment. She focused on the feel of Sweetie beneath her, on the hound's slow, steady breathing and the race of her heart in tandem with Jaslene's own. *We can do this.*

"Alright, riders! The rules are simple! No biting, gnashing, tail-whipping, kicking, stabbing, grappling, or maiming. No fireballs, enchantments, curses, or magical enhancements of any kind. Violation of any of these rules will result in an immediate disqualification! The first contestant to reach the 400-meter mark wins!"

The officiate shuffled off the track quickly, and the digital scoreboard at the side of the track lit up.

Riders and beasts alike burst into a frenzied shuffle as riders adjusted their positions and mounts tensed for the bell. Most had saddles and harnesses of some kind—except the centaur, of course—though the gargoyle rider used a cross between a harness and stirrups to perch on his companion's back, looking ridiculously like a toddler and parent.

Jaslene didn't use a saddle, either. Such contraptions would only hinder Sweetie's movement. With their psychic bond, Jaslene didn't need reins or riding crops to guide the Hellhound's path. Leaning forward, Jaslene gripped the long fur around Sweetie's ruff and squeezed her knees around the sturdy ribcage. Sweetie dropped into a crouch at the shift in weight, one paw forward as she waited for the signal to go.

The bell rang and the line of riders burst forward as one, the crowd screaming encouragement to their favorites. But these were not prized thoroughbreds trained for a life on the track. These were monsters of myth and magic trained simply to look impressive, if they were trained at all. It was immediately obvious running in close quarters with others they would normally see as enemies was not something any of the mounts were familiar with. Letting Sweetie focus on the running, Jaslene kept her attention on her opponents as chaos erupted across the track.

The chimera was the first to get cut. Overstimulated by the movement around it, all three heads whipped about in uncoordinated excitement. Rider Bob barked out a string of commands, but the chimera didn't even seem to remember he was there. The snake head swung around like a mace, smashing into the lion head. The lion head reared back in pain and anger, bashing the goat head right between the horns. The goat screamed and latched its jaw wholly around the snake in retaliation. Attacked on all sides, the chimera abandoned the race altogether in favor of defense mode, dropping into a barrel-roll to knock off whatever fierce predator had a hold on it. Bob's scream quickly turned to a gurgle under the weight of the massive, panicked beast.

Jaslene closed her eyes against the sound, grimacing at the easily avoidable accident. It wasn't enough to train a Veil creature—they were too wild for that. You had to bond with them, earn their trust so they wanted to follow you, or there was no predicting when they'd veer off to do their own thing. Many a trainer had met an unsightly end by forgetting one simple fact: if you have no power, you have no control. Bob had just learned that lesson the hard way.

The peryton sped to the head of the line on spindly legs, unimpeded by the slight weight of the gnome. Not to be outdone by a winged deer, Alistair urged Soul Crusher to a faster slither. The basilisk dutifully increased the speed of her undulating, her head pulling from side to side with enough force to snap the reins from the sorcerer's grip. In his desperate lunge to regain his hold, Alistair caught the strap of the mask by accident, yanking the covering from the basilisk's eyes in the process.

Free from the restraint, the basilisk set her glare on the immediate threat to her master's triumph and hissed. In the blink of an eye, the peryton froze in place, its momentum carrying the now-stone body into a head-over-heel stumble before crashing to the ground in a heap of rubble, the head of poor Thorn Berry skittering across the track like a macabre bowling ball.

Wails of outrage from the gnome's fan section echoed in Jaslene's ears as a horn blared and the officiate announced the disqualification of Alistair and Soul Crusher for breaking the "no maiming" rule.

Their odds of success increased by the timely exit of three opponents seemed to give a boost to the Marche Hare. The long-legged lagomorph dashed past Jaslene faster than any natural hare had a right to, the sprite whooping as she flashed by in a blur of fur and sparkles. No sooner had they taken the lead than the wyvern, unable to resist the temptation of such a luscious little snack, veered sharply off course to dive for the pair, maw wide.

The magician pulled on the harness and screamed for End Game to halt but, barred from magical methods of persuasion, he was unable to sway the huge reptile. The crowd surged to their feet with a roar of gasps, shuffling as close to the fence as they dared without risking injury themselves for a better view of the catastrophe unfurling on the field.

With a singular focus, the wyvern leapt for the hare, shoulder-checking the unicorn, who stumbled and tripped horn first into the centaur. The centaur screamed as the horn tore through his bicep and he dropped into a roll away from the unicorn and out of the race, blood splattering the sand on the track.

The unicorn recovered quickly, turning with preternatural agility on slim ankles to swerve around the wyvern and into first place. Heedless of the chaos around him, the wyvern barreled on after the hare, darting out his long neck to scoop up the speeding animal just as it crossed in front of the Hellhound on a path towards the bleachers and safety. Jaslene heard one high-pitched squeak before the beast's jaws snapped closed. Pye, who had abandoned her doomed mount and taken flight just nanoseconds before, now flew inches from the magician's face, bombarding him with a string of curses Jaslene had never heard before while he tried to nudge End Game off the track to no avail.

Her path now blocked by the happily munching (and disqualified) wyvern, Jaslene hunched over Sweetie's back and braced herself. The Hellhound lifted into the air in a smooth leap, clearing both the wyvern and his rider with ease before landing lightly on the sand without losing pace. The Witch swiveled to look over her shoulder at the remaining contestants.

The gryphon was loping along only a few feet behind, but the gap was widening. Designed for swooping and diving from above, the creature lost his edge on the ground and Jaslene could tell from the huffing and puffing his endurance was at an end. The gargoyle was faring no better, the weight of his companion on his shoulders adding to his already substantial bulk and hampering his movement. That left the unicorn as her only real competition.

Turning her head to the front, Jaslene estimated the unicorn would cross the finish line in just a handful of seconds. She had to overtake the mythical equine and her ethereal rider now, or go home with nothing to show for it but a wasted day. They could do this. Sweetie could do this. She trusted in her familiar more than she trusted in herself. She just had to push the hound a little more.

Tightening her grip on the ruff, Jaslene whispered harshly against the wind, "You let that blighted horse win and we're eating rice and beans for a week. No meat!"

The prospect of going without her preferred dish for so long provided more motivation for the oversized dog than any threat of violence ever could. Instantly, heat radiated from her coat, sweat beading up all over Jaslene's body from the sudden rise in temperature. Sweetie's legs lengthened, her frame growing taller and more sleek, the ears longer and the snout pointed. Murmurs of excitement rippled through the bleachers as Sweetie's eyes turned a vibrant glowing orange and yellow flames burst around her in a halo. The tendrils tickled at her flesh, but Jaslene remained unharmed. A Witch was never burned by the flames of her own familiar.

In her true shape, unencumbered by any glamor or effort to suppress her natural form to ease human sensibilities, Sweetie surged past the unicorn, the literal Fires of Hell trailing behind her and leaving perfect paw prints scorched in the dirt. Ringing bells of victory echoed over the field as the pair flew past the finish line in a blur of black and gold. The Hellhound slid to a stop amid a crescendo of whoops and hollers from the crowd and Jaslene collapsed against Sweetie's warm back with a sigh of relief. They won. They had actually won.

Slipping from her perch, Jaslene patted Sweetie, giving her a kiss on the snoot as the flames died down and the Hellhound sat on her haunches to rest. The unicorn rider pulled her mount up close, dismounted and reached her hand out to Jaslene.

"Well done," Blythe Gwinny congratulated. "Can't say I'm thrilled to be second place, but at least I got the chance to see a Hellhound in full glory."

Jaslene accepted the compliment gratefully and turned to wave at the still-cheering crowd, who rewarded her attention by increasing the volume even more. The officiate trotted over, bullhorn in one hand, big golden trophy in the other.

"Congratulations to our first ever winner of the Grym Dash and a real underdog, Jaslene and her Hellhound Sweetie!"

Jaslene took the proffered trophy, holding it up for all to see, smiling wide at the thought of all her bills disappearing—at least for this month.

"What do you plan on doing with the prize money?" the officiate asked, holding the bullhorn close to Jaslene's face to catch her reply.

She didn't even have to think about it. The answer had been at the forefront of her mind since she first saw the flyer.

"Pay my rent!"

HOME BREW

Artymos Morely hovered his nose over the glass bottle and breathed deep. Tart with just a hint of musk. He didn't know if the musky smell was normal or if it had gone bad from sitting on the shelf too long. No matter. He supposed it'd work either way.

Gently tipping the bottle, watching carefully as the thick purple liquid oozed down the neck to drip into the cauldron, Arty counted out three drops and swiftly lifted the bottle away. That ought to do it. He could always add more if he felt like it.

The purple drops melted into the bubbling brew. Arty stirred the liquid with a slender stick, wondering at the way the tiny swirls of purple blended into the dark green and added a golden shimmer to the surface.

He leaned over and took a whiff, detecting the subtle change in scent from old pond scum to old pond scum with a hint of perfume. Yes, he was getting closer now.

Turning back to the row of shelves behind him, Arty replaced the bottle and scanned the labels for the next ingredient. Many of the bottles hadn't been touched in ages, thick dust obscured the carefully written words. He rubbed his thumb along the labels to read his mother's large and flowing script. He squinted in an effort to recall the basic alchemy lessons his mother had forced him to sit through, the long-ago lessons a jumble in the dredges of his memory. With a shake of his head, he turned away from the shelves.

It was like reading another language. He should have paid more attention—his livelihood depended on it—but reading and learning had always been difficult for Arty. It was boring and he couldn't keep his focus for more than a few minutes before his mind wandered towards daydreams and musings. He'd much rather be with his father on the other side of the shop, helping customers sift through the latest trinkets brought in from the city or upholstering artfully carved furniture in supple fabrics. Using his hands came much more naturally to him than using his brain.

He leaned over the worn counter that separated his father's sundry goods from his mother's apothecary nook and flipped through the large tome resting on the scarred surface. He was almost there, he could feel it. Just a few more ingredients and he'd have the right concoction.

A slender black cat leapt onto the counter with a soft mew. She padded over on tiny feet and pushed her head against Arty's arm. He waved her away.

"Go on, Stilda, I'm working."

Stilda meowed back, louder, and tapped his hand with her paw. He glared at her, sliding his hand out of her reach. Why did she have to be so bothersome when he was working? Didn't she know how important this was?

"Go chase mice or something."

With an angry switch of her tail, the cat jumped to the floor, trotting away between the barrels of pickles and bolts of last year's fabrics. Arty shook his head and sighed, turning back to the book. He wiped a hand over his face, tired of reading, tired of trying to accomplish such an impossible task. He glanced up at the clock, the hands just visible between twigs of elderberry and bunches of bayberry hung on the wall to dry. One hour remained before his parents were due back home. One hour to finish this droll task or be grounded for at least a decade by his father.

He turned the page with an angry flick of his fingers, inwardly cursing himself for getting into this predicament. If he made it out of this mess unscathed, he promised to pay more attention during his mother's lectures.

His eyes scanned the page, lighting upon a useful-looking entry.

Yba Bulb greatly increases overall health and works well as an accelerator in most tinctures and potions. It is best used when reduced to a thick paste.

Aha, yes. That was it. That's the final ingredient.

Snatching the jar of Yba Bulb paste from the shelf behind him, Arty scooped a generous portion out with a long-handled spoon and stirred the paste into the gold-green mixture. The bubbling increased, large droplets clearing the rim of the cauldron to sizzle on the table. Arty stepped back from the scalding droplets, twisting the knob on the portable burner to lower the flame. Too much heat with an accelerator could be explosive and Arty had enough problems at the moment without adding "potion volcano" to the list of messes to clean up. Once the roiling surface had calmed to a simmer, he resumed stirring the concoction, careful not to let it burn to the bottom of the pot.

Perfumed pond scum evolved into sweet and sour, making his mouth water. It was a move in the right direction, but he still didn't have it quite right.

Stilda was at his feet again, rubbing her side along his leg. He glanced down at the cat.

"I'm working on it. You know I've never been very good at this. I think I've almost got it, though. Still smells a bit off. I'm not sure what I'm missing."

"Meow."

"I know, but I've tried everything."

The cat sat back on her haunches, gazing up at him with large green eyes. Arty pursed his lips and turned away from the vexing feline.

"Don't look at me like that. You knew what you were getting into."

Arty stepped around Stilda and studied the book again. He flipped through several pages, but didn't find anything useful. He groaned, pulling at a hank of black hair in frustration.

"Just one more thing, I know it!"

An insistent tugging at his leg drew his attention once more to the sable-haired cat. She stretched up along his leg, reaching her paws as high as she could manage, the tips of her claws snagging on his canvas pants.

"Meow!"

"Be patient," Arty groused, gently pushing her away with his knee so as not to hurt her. "I just need to think."

Stilda howled louder, more insistent. Taking a few light steps towards the large window at the end of the shelves, the cat paused to look over her shoulder and call again. Arty slammed the spoon down with a moan, rolling his eyes at the feline's persistent nagging.

"What, Stilda? You want a treat? Do you need out?"

The cat narrowed her eyes at his patronizing tone, and Arty snapped his mouth shut. He felt the heat of shame rising to his cheeks and he mumbled an apology.

Stilda accepted his apology with a little trill and sprinted towards the window. Leaping up onto the ledge, she nudged a hairbrush with her head, looking at Arty before nudging it again. With his brow creasing into a perplexed frown, Arty stepped over to inspect the brush. What was Stilda trying to tell him?

Long strands of thick black hair wrapped around the bristles in a tangled mass. It was much too long to belong to Arty or his father, and too dark to be his mother's. That meant it must be his sister's hair trapped in the brush. He gasped, realization dawning on his inattentive mind. Snatching up the brush, he scurried back over to the cauldron, Stilda tight on his heels.

Pulling a few strands from the bristles, Arty dropped them into the bubbling cauldron. He stirred briskly, smiling broadly as the scent of cinnamon wafted up on the steam. He shuffled his feet, nearly jumping up and down in his excitement. This was it. He'd done it!

Dipping the spoon into the thick brew, Arty scooped up as much as he could and slowly knelt on one knee. Careful not to spill, he held the bowl of the spoon towards the cat. Stilda took a hesitant step closer, delicately sniffing at the potion with a twitching pink nose. Rolling her eyes one last time to Arty, she lowered her head and lapped at the offering.

With a choking, gurgling sound, the cat stumbled back from the spoon, shaking her head like she had a bone stuck in her maw. Falling to her side, Stilda convulsed, her black legs jerking and twitching alarmingly. Arty took a step back, watching the seizing cat with concern and anticipation.

The fur on her flank began to roil and expand, as if a snake slithered beneath the inky surface. It swelled and swelled until her side literally split, the fur rolling away as a pale mass burst forth. The form grew until it was nearly as tall as Arty, all black and white and pink. In a matter of seconds, his sister stood before him, her mass of long black hair swirling around her shoulders, the pink maxi dress she wore no worse for wear.

Arty smiled, offering a timid wave.

"He-ey. See? I fixed it. Don't tell Mom."

The green eyes that met his burned with fury, and his smile faltered. Stilda's hand slapped against his cheek with enough force to cut his lip on a tooth. Arty didn't retaliate; he couldn't deny he deserved it.

"Don't you ever do that to me again!"

SPHINX JINX

The crew bustled around the stage, making last minute adjustments to lighting and props. Kiza bounced on her heels, the ball of apprehension in the pit of her stomach sending bolts of energy through her limbs. The djinn tugged on a long black braid and wiped sweat from her blue-skinned brow. Next to her, the sphinx Nara patiently waited while the make-up artist highlighted her golden cheekbones and smoothed brown feathers back into place along pert wings. The hairstylist twisted the long, honey-gold mane into a chignon and brushed loose fur from her hide.

The sphinx rolled a tawny eye at her handler, sharp canines peeking from between bright red lips.

"Your anxious prancing is distracting. Calm yourself, I will not lose."

She glanced over at the show's first contestant being similarly preened on the other side of the stage. He was middle-aged and balding, with a paunch grown from too much beer and too little exercise.

The sphinx sighed, flexing her toes so the nails protruded to their full, alarming length before retracting back into a relaxed pose. "I do wish they had provided a leaner one. These Americans give me heartburn."

Kiza blanched under her cerulean hue.

"You cannot eat him, Nara," she whispered harshly, pinning a warning glare on the creature. "This is a game. If you win, he merely goes home without any treasure."

Nara scoffed, smiling at her the way one would at an ill-informed child.

"That is not how the game is played. I have done this many times, Kiza," she assured her handler in bored nonchalance. "The game is mine."

Her stomach turned cold. Her greatest fear about this whole game show fiasco was quickly becoming reality. Whose idea was it anyway to hire a real live sphinx to host a trivia show? These silly people cared for nothing but gimmicks and the bottom line. They didn't understand the nature of a sphinx, their bloodlust and obsession with proving their superiority at brainteasers.

Kiza should never have let it get this far. She told Kevin, their boss at Extravaganza Circus, to refuse to loan Nara out to the show. The fee, however, had been too much for Kevin to refuse. The producers wanted a Grym monster, but did it have to be a real sphinx? Her boss could easily have told the faerie Meegan to give them an illusion, one that would film real enough without the danger of tangible claws and teeth, or find a shapeshifter capable of holding the guise for extended periods of time.

It was too late now. The deal had been struck, the contracts signed. Kiza and Nara were to film eight episodes or risk litigation. Kiza didn't think they'd last even one.

Catching sight of Mr. Davidson just off-stage, she rushed over to reason with the trend-savvy businessman one last time. She grabbed his elbow and tugged, forcing him to look her in the eye.

"Please, Mr. Davidson, you cannot do this. Nara is not a pet, and she does not think like you humans. The game is real for her."

He jerked his arm from her grasp, smoothing wrinkles the djinn's thin blue fingers had left in the bespoke fabric. His smile was bland, businesslike, and not nearly as concerned as he should be.

"Perfect. A bit of realism to liven up the crowd. They love off-the-cuff banter."

"This is serious. She cannot host. Can't you use an illusion instead?"

Mr. Davidson narrowed his eyes, glancing over at Nara in the final stages of wardrobe with uncertainty. He pursed his lips, recalling the huge investments his company had laid on the venture. VeilFilm Enterprises was counting on a Grym celebrity success to rejuvenate their failing empire. It was critical the sphinx deliver not only otherworldly flare, but charisma and flawless performance.

"Why? Did she forget her lines?" He shook the too-late concern from his mind. "Don't worry, we've got cue cards in case she stumbles. Everything will go smoothly."

"Mr. Davidson-"

"Look, the cameras are about to roll. Can she say her lines, or not?"

Her efforts clearly wasted, Kiza sighed, her shoulders slumping as she abandoned warning the stage manager of the impending doom.

"Yes, but that is not the problem."

"Great, good enough. Places, everyone!"

In a flurry of movement, the brilliant lights flicked on and stage-hands ghosted behind fake walls as the cameras began rolling. Kiza chewed her fingernails from the sidelines, fighting the urge to run across the stage and demand they give up. Nara sat elegantly on a silk-draped ottoman, eyeing the first contestant with a wicked twinkle. The balding man, jittery with the excitement of being on TV, pulled at the collar of his suit, sweat from the hot lights already beading up on his pasty scalp. The live audience clapped at the prompt. As the sound died down, Nara turned to the camera.

"Welcome to Riddle Me This, where contestants answer riddles for a chance to win cash prizes. I'm your host, Nara the Sphinx. Competing with me today is John Fenwick from Cleveland, Ohio. John, would you tell the audience a bit about yourself?"

John cleared his throat noisily, pulling on his collar again. He coughed and leaned over the microphone that rose from the padded pedestal.

"I'm an HR manager from Cleveland. I enjoy fly-fishing, football, and reality TV. I'd like to give a shout-out to my wife Carrie, and my boss Jim. Sorry I called in sick today."

His laughter sounded contrived, as did the complimentary giggles from the crowd. Recognizing the cue to smile, Nara pulled her lips back in an imitation of a human grin. Her teeth flashed in the light, curved and sharp, but her eyes watched the contestant with a hungry glint. The man's smile faltered and he leaned away from Nara, eyes wide. Kiza pressed a hand over her mouth to stifle a groan. She looked around at the crew patiently watching near her. Not a single one seemed to realize the precariousness of the situation.

"Let me explain the rules for our audience. You will be asked three riddles for prizes totaling more than $40,000. You will have fifteen seconds to answer each riddle. You will be given a chance after each question to take your winnings and leave. If you get even one question wrong, you lose everything. Are you ready?"

His fear washed away by the promise of cash, John nodded his head. His eyes darted from the camera to the live audience, then to Nara.

"Yes. I can do this. Go Bobcats!"

A digital screen behind Nara came to life, displaying a countdown clock in bold letters and a prize box labeled $1000.

"This first riddle is for $1000. *Feed me and I live. Yet, give me a drink, and I die. What am I?* You have fifteen seconds."

The countdown began, a loud ticking sound accompanying each passing second. John scoffed, smirking at the crowd.

"That one's easy. Fire."

A bell rang across the auditorium, signaling the correct answer. The audience clapped, John fist-pumping the air. He looked at Nara, smug and pleased with his easy win. Nara gazed back, unimpressed. From beyond the camera's view, Kiza released a breath.

"Congratulations. You have $1000. Is that enough for you, or do you want more? Remember, if you get this next one wrong, you lose."

"I'll keep going. I think I can win."

"As you wish. This next riddle is for $10,000. *You will always find me in the past. I can be created in the present, but the future can never taint me. What am I?*"

John shifted his feet, rolled his eyes to the ceiling. He murmured to himself, scratched his shining pate. The crowd twittered, abuzz with the possibility the game might already be over. Kiza twisted her hands, teeth clenching her lip as her heart pounded. *Please don't let him get it wrong.*

"You have ten seconds. Eight."

"Oh, I got it! History!"

John jumped in the air, yelling his elation at correctly guessing the second riddle. The enthusiastic cheering of the crowd ricocheted off the walls. Relief flooded through Kiza, leaving her weak and she leaned against a wall to hold herself up. She pressed one slim hand against her chest in an effort to slow her heart. She closed her eyes, offering a prayer up to whatever god controlled this blasted dimension. Only one more question remained.

The screen at the front of the seats flashed the command for the audience to settle down. When the last of the clapping had ceased, Nara turned back to John.

"Another correct answer. You are doing marvelously well. You have $11,000. Are you satisfied, or do you wish to continue?"

"Let's go, baby! This is easier than I thought!"

A slow smile spread across Nara's face, and Kiza straightened with a curse. She knew that smile. It was the same look Nara had just before she swallowed a meal whole. The rules may state John would simply leave, but riddles were serious business to sphinxes. One did not dangle the promise of fresh meat in front of a sphinx and not deliver, especially when it had won a battle of wits. It wasn't a pleasant distraction but a point of pride.

Kiza stepped over to Mr. Davidson. She had to put an end to this now, before the unsuspecting man became an afternoon snack.

"Mr. Davidson, please. You have to stop the show. Nara will win."

Mr. Davidson shushed her, patting her on the head like a small child. He sneered, giving her a mocking wink, as he leaned close to her.

"This is great. They're building tension. We can't have it look too easy."

"She's going to eat him!"

"Don't be ridiculous. This is TV, it's all just for fun. Nara knows the rules."

"She only knows *her* rules."

Mr. Davidson ignored her insistent warning, waving at an assistant to pull Kiza away from him. The djinn groaned in frustration, but allowed herself to be guided back to her spot. She turned her attention to the stage, every muscle in her body tensed.

"Do you wish to be challenged? I have one more riddle left, and I can promise you it will be challenging. Do you still wish to continue? If you cannot answer, you lose."

John shook his head, swinging his arms and bouncing on his feet with restrained excitement.

"Nah, I got this. Let's go. For the win, baby!"

"For $30,000, I offer you the final riddle. *An old man wished to leave all of his money to one of his three sons, but didn't know which he should give it to. He gave each a few coins and told them to buy something that would be able to fill their room. The first man bought straw, but it was not enough to fill the room. The second bought sticks, but they also did not fill the room. The third man bought two things that filled the room, so he obtained his father's fortune. What were the two things that the man bought?*"

The question was an old one, popular centuries ago. John frowned as he struggled for an answer. The ticking of the clock echoed ominously. The tension of the crowd became palpable as each second ticked by without an answer. John repeated his nervous dance, becoming more agitated as time grew shorter. Nara grinned, adjusting her paws beneath her chest, her shoulders bunching as she prepared to win. Her hind feet flexed in anticipation, making her haunches dance under the spotlights.

"Eight seconds."

John thumped a fist on the pedestal, growling his frustration. He peered into the audience as if expecting to find the answer on their nervous faces. Kiza stretched her back and shoulders, unclenching her hands and shaking the stiffness from the joints. She took a step forward, bracing herself for the inevitable intervention.

"Five seconds."

He swung his head back around to Nara, still at a loss. He met her eager glare, watched her lips lick a trickle of saliva from the corner of her mouth. Thick claws dug into the ottoman as she slowly adjusted her position. It was almost time.

John whimpered, wringing his hands. He stuttered a few half-formed pleas. His lower lip trembled with the beginning of a sob, eyeing the tension of the sphynx's powerful muscles. Kiza could see the regret on his face, the fear gripping his body. It was easy to forget the danger Grym creatures presented on something as benign as a game show, to think the presence of an audience and cameras would prevent disaster. Her warnings about Nara's capricious nature had gone ignored, and they were all about to learn just how hazardous a Grym could be.

The timer hit zero, the resounding buzz loud and piercing. John startled, still staring at Nara in growing alarm. The audience gasped in disappointment, emanating murmurs of sympathy with the would-be champion.

"You lose," Nara announced, springing from her perch towards the frightened man with claws outstretched.

John screamed as the leonine nails perforated soft flesh, the weight of her body knocking him to the ground. His scream ended in gurgling, limbs flailing, Nara's canines gripping the curve of his neck tight.

Panic erupted across the audience. Deafening screams filled the auditorium as the crowd surged to their feet, scrambling to flee the building. Staff stood transfixed by the impossible scene for a split second before leaping into action. Most fled, pushing their way into the stampeding crowd. A brave few grabbed light poles, chairs, anything within reach, in an attempt to scare Nara away from her prey.

Nara roared, adjusting her stance to tower over her prize. She stood on his chest to hold him, one large paw sweeping past the heads of the staff members as a warning. Beneath her, John cried and pleaded for help, blood gushing from the wound on his neck, thick fingers pushing ineffectively at golden-furred legs.

Kiza rushed forward, careful to stay behind Nara. She needed the advantage of surprise to ensnare a sphinx in full hunting mode. Though their poking and prodding served only to anger the creature, the staff provided a much needed distraction. Focused on defending her prize, Nara failed to notice her handler taking position behind her.

Kiza set her feet shoulder-width apart, her upper body leaned back in anticipation of the struggle. Clapping her hands together, she spoke the words of Power and a long shimmering rope of golden light issued from her palms. She faced her palms out towards Nara, the ends of the rope sailing across the stage. Nara reared, screeching her anger as the magical ropes wrapped around her limbs, beneath her chest and curling up to bind her jaw. Kiza flicked her wrists, twisting the rope around her forearms for a better hold, and yanked. Several moments of pulling, straining, and twisting followed before Kiza had drug Nara far enough away from John that the staff could pull him to safety.

Pulling a magically enhanced taser from her holster, Kiza delivered two quick jolts to Nara's hip. The sphinx collapsed with a pained grunt and Kiza knelt to check her vitals. The pulse was strong, her breathing even. She replaced the taser with a sigh, disappointed she'd been forced to rely on its use.

The paramedics arrived, outfitting John with oxygen and bandages. He had lost a lot of blood but with quick treatment, his injuries should not be fatal. He cried weakly as they lifted him onto a stretcher.

On the other side of the stage, Mr. Davidson pressed a cellphone to his ear, his speech urgent, hands waving in distress.

"You need to get his wife on the phone right now and clean this mess up. Pay her whatever she wants. We can't afford a scandal right now. And set up a press conference. I need to spin the narrative quick before the rumors get out."

Kiza plopped down on the ground next to Nara, waiting for the frenzy of activity to die down before trying to move the sphinx. She smiled as she wove her braid in and out of her fingers, humming a light tune. They'd be sent home now, back to the security of the Circus. Kevin would huff and puff and demand to know how Kiza could let this happen, but he'd blow himself out quickly. Nara would be back where she belonged, corralled behind thick glass and heavy ward runes. And they'd never see Mr. Davidson or a television studio again.

A Reap of Faith

Fish stood over the crumpled body, glaring at the lifeless corpse with a mix of agitation and sympathy. The man's disembodied spirit stared down at his earthly remains in confused bewilderment, shuffling as if contemplating making a break for it. Fish glanced from the spirit beside him to its former body on the ground and sighed.

"Why do you always do this, Helen?"

Hovering on Fish's other side, Helen shrugged. Or, at least Fish thought she did. It was difficult to tell what she was doing beneath the heavy black shroud which concealed everything but the pale, bony hands that clutched the slender scythe. Fish sighed again.

Rolling his head towards the spirit, he asked, "What's your name, corpse?"

"Corpse?" The man choked on the word, ogling Fish as one would a particularly nasty-looking spider.

"No, no, you have to pick a name," Fish snapped irritably. "I can't keep calling you Corpse. It's too confusing."

The man's mouth flapped several times before he managed to stutter, "Dave. My name is—was—Dave."

"Alright, Dave. This is what we like to call in the Underworld a right royal cock-up. Helen, bless your worm-eaten little pea-brain, you've done it again. *For the ninth time.*"

"You make it sound like I do this sort of thing all the time," Helen whispered back, her face the usual hole of shapeless blackness.

Fish hated her face. He hated trying to talk to someone who didn't even have eyes. How was he supposed to know if they were paying attention if they didn't have eyes?

"The ninth time, Helen," Fish repeated sternly.

The Reaper waved one skeletal hand blithely. "In two hundred years. That doesn't sound so bad."

Fish growled, gnashing his teeth. His feet lifted off the ground in a slight bounce with each clipped word. "Nine times, Helen! You get nine chances before you're booted right back to Hell, and this is the ninth time!"

He shut his mouth abruptly, taking a deep breath. Licking the back of one white-dipped paw, Fish leisurely slicked it along one side of his head, from eyebrow to just behind one long ear. Again. Again. It was calming, and he desperately needed calm. He felt the erratic twitching of his tail slow, the fur along his spine settle. He could be calm. He could think of a plan.

Fish has been dead for a very long time, drowned when an irate shopkeeper stuffed him in a sack and tossed him in the Thames for rummaging in his garbage bins. It hadn't been pleasant. Finding out his final destination was Hell had been no nap in the sun, either. All that screaming. The horrid smells. The fire. Not a single quiet corner in the place. He must have gone decades without any decent sleep.

When Death offered him an opportunity to escape the stench of his own singed fur, Fish had jumped at the chance. If he assisted the Reapers in their task for five hundred years, he'd be reborn. It had been his bad luck to be assigned to Helen, the most bungling, addle-brained Reaper he'd ever had the misfortune to know.

They had one task: collect the souls of those whose time had come and direct them to their proper afterlife. For any other Veil Walker, it should have been a cakewalk. Unfortunately, Helen couldn't tell the difference between someone cloaked in the pall of death and, well, any other human. Now, they were stuck with Dave, out of chances, and Fish still 277 years short of rebirth.

"Am I dead, then?" Dave asked. "Is this the Afterlife?"

Fish rolled his golden eyes. Why were the recently departed so dense?

"No." He gestured to their surroundings with a graceful spin. "This is an alleyway. Helen and I will be escorting you to your personalized Afterlife shortly, as we march ourselves *right back to the depths of Hades*."

Fish's voice rose with each word until it ricocheted off the brick walls in a piercing screech that made Dave wince. Narrowing his eyes at the nervous spirit, Fish turned away with a snort and trotted across the alleyway to where a disheveled man slumped against a dumpster. He stopped at the man's feet, flicking at the needle still dangling from the unconscious man's arm.

"It's very simple, Helen. Sickly chap having an overdose." He leapt to perch on the back of Dave's body. "Healthy guy out for a walk. How did you mess this up?"

"He was in the right place. This was the spot I was supposed to Reap. He was in *the spot*."

"You can't just snatch the first soul you see! Critical thinking, Helen!"

Dave watched the exchange silently, slowly angling his head from one to the other. The shock of his sudden death lingered, which Fish much preferred over hysteria.

Helen shrugged again. "I could just put him right back in there. His body hasn't been dead long."

Fish gasped in mock delight, ears and tail high. His tone dripped with sarcasm. "Oh, could you? That would be just swell."

Helen rotated to face Dave, gesturing to his body with a sweep of her free hand, inclining her head politely.

Dave frowned at the silent specter, then jumped as her implied request filtered through. "Oh, you want me to stand over my body?"

"Yes, please, Dave," Fish snapped, leaving his perch with a graceful leap to stand by Helen's side. "Just stand over there real still and Helen will pop you right back in and we can forget this unpleasant episode ever happened."

Dave nodded dully. "Yeah, sure."

Moving to stand at the head of his prone form, Dave turned and waited. The cat's shoulders relaxed and the tension left his jaw. It would all be over soon and back to work as usual. There was no reason to panic. Only 277 more years to go.

Helen remained motionless, and the silence dragged. Fish coughed to propel his partner into action. The Reaper shuffled, adjusting the scythe to the front, her shadowed face pointed towards Dave with an air of concentration. Nothing happened. Dave bounced on his heels, grimacing awkwardly. Fish felt the hair on his spine rise again as his nervousness rose. He patted at Helen's knee.

"What's wrong? Pop him back in before his organs turn to mush."

The shoulders beneath the heavy robe slumped. "Give me a minute. I have to remember how."

Fish sprung to all fours. "What do you mean, *how*? Just reverse whatever it is you do to pull them out. Soul out, soul in."

The hooded head shook and she turned the blank hollow of a face to him. "It's not a Jack-in-the-Box. If I do it wrong, his spirit won't stick."

He bared his teeth and growled. "Why did you say you could 'pop him back in' if you don't know how? Are you trying to give me a stroke?"

She waved a hand dismissively. "I know how. I just have to remember."

His complaint of a stroke was meant to be hyperbolic but at the moment, Fish truly felt a vein on the verge of bursting. His whole body rumbled with fury, his vision washing over in white hot rage. Of all the Reapers in all the universes, why did he have to be saddled with the only one who couldn't tell her scythe from her foot?

"Uh, guys?" Dave whispered.

Fish ignored the twitchy spirit. He had no patience for existential crises right now.

"You figure out how to put Dave back right now or so help me, Helen, I will leave dead mice in your skull hole every day for a millennium!"

Dave screamed, a sound of sheer frenzied distress. Fish turned just in time to see what he had confused for the symptoms of an encroaching apoplexy was in fact a large diesel truck barreling down the alley. Dave's body, flat against the ground and clad in dark clothes, lay below the beam of the headlights, unnoticed. Fish shivered at the uncomfortable shock as the truck passed through their not-really-there forms, and right over Dave's body. The tires tore through soft flesh with a sickening squelch, the driver slamming on the brakes at the unexpected bump.

The driver hopped out and rushed to examine the corpse in a panic as the three incorporeal beings stared at the mangled, useless remains spread out before them. Dave sunk to his knees with a wail, vainly trying to shove his body parts back together with hands that could no longer touch the mortal world. His back arched, tail fully poofed, Fish paced in a circle, canines grinding into his lower lip.

"Can you fix this, Helen? Huh? Can you?" He let out a frustrated yowl, abruptly halting to raise one leg straight above his ears and groom a spot on the back of his thigh. The usually cathartic action did nothing to relieve his stress. He returned to his pacing.

Helen straightened her shoulders, bringing the scythe upright. She turned her face towards Fish, the blackness beaming at him triumphantly.

"I remember how to put him back."

The last shred of his sanity snapped. With a vicious growl, Fish leapt, claws first, at the Reaper's hood.

— ◇ —

Once Fish had expended his fury on Helen's robes, a weary calm settled over him. He was left exhausted and drained, his shoulders drooping with the weight of his disappointment. Dave had finally cried himself out, a small favor considering their predicament. The alleyway flooded with flashing lights and emergency crew, unwittingly passing back and forth through the incorporeal beings. The tingling of his flesh each time a body passed through him grated on his nerves. Fish shuffled out of the way, joined by Helen and Dave along one brick wall. The trio stood watching the ambulance crew scrape Dave's body off the pavement and into a slick black bag.

"I can't believe this is happening to me," Dave muttered.

"Well, this is it," Fish sighed. "Turn in your scythe, it's back to Hell we go."

Dave turned to Fish with bulging eyes, his ghostly face paling. His voice, when he managed to speak, was high and strained.

"Am I going to Hell?"

Fish sighed again and spun in a circle several times before settling back on his haunches. He began licking one paw, speaking between each swipe of his tongue.

"No. Maybe. I don't know. You died too early, so you'll go to a holding place until they decide what to do with you."

"Like a waiting room? Is it pleasant? No elevator music, is there? I hate elevator music. It puts me to sleep."

Fish ignored the rambled questions, turning to Helen and tugging on her hem with his freshly cleaned claws.

"Come on, then. Guess it's time to face the music. The big boss-man will find out sooner or later, anyway."

Fish flipped on his heel and trotted down the alley towards the darkened corners nestled in the dead end. Shadows were the portals to Limbo, the pathways Reapers took to travel all over the globe in an instant. He waited for the telltale *clink-clink* of Helen's scythe behind him, but all he could hear was Dave following along mumbling to himself.

Half-turning to glance over his shoulder, he saw Helen still in the same place, staring blankly at the chalk outline that marked where Dave's body had been. He half-turned around, yowling when the inattentive Dave kicked him in the flanks. Mortals may walk through them as if they were air, but they were solid enough to each other.

"No point dawdling, Helen. Hurry up and let's get this over with."

The Reaper raised her blank hooded face to his.

"Does it have to be *his* body?"

"What?" He heard her well enough, though Helen rarely spoke above a whisper. He just couldn't understand the question.

"The soul. Does it have to go back into its original body, or will any old form do? The only thing that matters is that the soul is *alive*. Right?"

Fish squinted, trying to recall the dry and much too long seminar he'd been forced to attend centuries ago. A soul had to have a body to stay on earth, that was obvious. But he couldn't recall any specific rules about whether it had to be the *original* body. And if Dave had a body, he wouldn't have to go to the Afterlife and they wouldn't lose their jobs.

With a short, joyful cackle, Fish hopped and spun in a circle. "Helen, I think you might be on to something."

"You mean, I don't have to be dead? You can bring me back to life?"

Helen nodded. "In a manner of speaking, yes. You won't be Dave anymore. You'll take over the new body's life."

Dave brushed aside her words with a wave of his hand. "But I'll be alive. How do we do that?"

"Find the next guy in line, Reap him and shove you in his spot before his organs go bad," Fish explained. He could barely contain his excitement now. Helen's suggestion had renewed his outlook on Eternity.

The revelation this didn't have to be the end had Dave bouncing on his heels. "Yeah, alright. Cool. So, who's next?"

Helen reached inside her robes with her free hand, pulling out the slim tablet issued to all Reapers for tracking their next target. She flicked it on and scrolled through the waiting list with one bony finger.

"Too old. Too young. No. No. How about that one?"

She bent over to allow Fish a glance at the screen. He ignored her and took another excited turn.

"Fine time to be worried about choosing appropriate targets, Helen. Just pick one."

With a shrug, the Reaper replaced the tablet in the folds of fabric and started for the shadowy corner, Fish and Dave close behind. The moment they stepped into the black void of shadows, they emerged out the other side into a small living room decorated in soft pastels and overstuffed furniture. A woman reclined on the paisley sofa, a glass of wine in one hand and a tissue in the other as an old Rene Zelleweger flick played on the TV.

"Ugh, my sister made me watch this one," Dave began, following Helen to hover behind the sofa. "Never really cared for these sappy movies. Hey, lady, are you alright?"

The wine glass thunked to the carpet, a pink stain spreading across the beige pile as the woman leaned forward, wheezing heavily with a hand to her chest. She reached out with her other hand, fumbling for the cellphone on the side table, beads of sweat bursting across her brow.

Dave darted around Helen, making a grab for the cellphone and emitted a bark of dismay as his hand went right through it, table and all.

"Aren't we going to help her?" he demanded at the silently waiting Helen.

Fish let out a bored yawn. "We are helping," he replied, examining the nails on one paw for stray hairs. Not finding any, he gave it a quick lick nonetheless, just to be sure. "No phone call will save her tonight."

Exhausted, face red and swollen from struggling to breathe, the woman let her arm drop and fell back against the cushions, eyes rolling up in silent pleading. Helen reached down with one hand and gently tapped the woman's shoulder. Instantly, her face relaxed and her body went limp as what little air that remained in her lungs rushed out in a soft whisper.

Not a moment later, her spirit appeared next to Helen, glancing around her living room like she'd never seen it before.

"Hello, welcome to the Afterlife," Fish greeted, wrapping his body around the woman's ankles and herding her gently towards a corner of the room. "This way, please."

A circle of dazzling light appeared in the corner, growing larger and larger until a tunnel tall enough for the woman to pass through had formed, glowing with an almost fluorescent yet somehow welcoming glare.

The woman dug her heels in at the sight of the tunnel, pushing back against Fish, who yowled in irritation and hopped out of the way.

"Wait. What?" She glanced back over her shoulder to Helen and her newly vacated body now slumped on the sofa. She pointed to her mortal remains with an indignant huff. "Did I just die?"

"Surprise!" Fish chirped, then gave her ankle a soft swipe. "Now, go down the hall. Someone will explain it all to you."

The spirit sidestepped Fish's attempts to nudge her closer to the light. "Why can't you explain it to me?"

Dave snorted. "Lady, I've been dead for a couple hours and I still don't get it."

"Very helpful, Dave," Fish hissed between clenched teeth. Turning back to the woman, he gestured to the tunnel with a shake of his head. "Just trot along, now. Everything will be fine."

The woman glanced down at Fish, lips twisting at being asked to trust a talking cat, then up at Dave, who shrugged. Finally, she turned her face to Helen. With a sage nod and a slowly pointing finger, the Reaper motioned for the spirit to enter the light. Nodding in resignation, the woman turned and marched into the tunnel, the opening shrinking with each step she took until it was gone from the mortal realm completely.

Fish gave an irritated sigh. "Every single time. I tell them exactly what's what and it's 'oh, what's going on' and 'I can't go into the light'. One idiot wave from you, and off they go."

"It's the hood," Helen replied. "Makes me enigmatic. Humans like that."

"Humans also like peanut butter and mayonnaise sandwiches, so their judgement is suspect."

The black-robed shoulder rose and fell in a shrug and she turned her empty cowl to Dave. "I can put you in, now."

Dave scoffed and pointed at the woman's corpse. "What, in there? It's a woman."

The Reaper cocked her head to the side at his offended tone, and Dave flapped his arms as if the reason for his offense should have been obvious. With an annoyed sigh, Fish leapt to the back of the sofa and pushed his head against the back of Dave's hand.

"It'll be a new adventure. You'll learn new skills. Try new things."

The spirit's eyes just about bugged out of his head and his voice rose an octave. "She's just had a heart attack!"

Fish tried to snort, but it turned into a sneeze. The unexpected and undignified squeak that escaped his nose rattled his fur and Fish spun in an agitated circle.

"So, go to the doctor. Eat right. Get some exercise. You'll do fine."

"But couldn't you have found me a man?" the spirit whined, his whole body bouncing like a toddler about to throw a tantrum.

Fish lost all semblance of pleading and niceness. "Are you getting in or not?"

Dave frowned as he weighed his options. "Maybe. I mean, no, I don't think so. Not a woman. I'm just not comfortable with it. I mean, what if she's someone's mother or girlfriend? Too awkward."

Little white canines glinted in the light as Fish's lips curled. "Fine," he snarled. "No women. Helen, who's next?"

Helen lolled her head in a half circle in just such a way Fish knew she was rolling her eyes at him—if she had eyes. Bracing her scythe over her shoulder, she again consulted her tablet briefly.

"Well, it is a male. But I'm not sure it's up to Dave's standards."

"Why?" Dave asked. "What's wrong with him?"

"Does it matter?" Fish snapped, hopping down from the sofa and herding the pair towards a shadowed doorway. "It's the requested gender, that's good enough. Beggars can't be choosers, Dave. Be reasonable, now. Come on."

◆―◆―◆

"This is not reasonable."

Fish made the cat version of a shrug. "Well, he didn't have a heart attack, at least."

"It's a dog."

"A male dog."

"He's quite fluffy," Helen chimed in, scratching the husky's specter behind the ears.

Dave's head shot up from the body of the grey and white husky to glare at the Reaper doting over the canine's spirit form. "You really are the dumbest Reaper there is, aren't you? How could you possibly think I'd want to live as a dog?"

"All life is precious, Dave, no matter its form. Besides, what's not to enjoy? Free food, a warm home, all the pats and treats you could want and never have to work again. Sounds lucky to me."

"He choked on a bone! How lucky is that?"

"I have to agree with him there, Helen," Fish quipped.

He hopped towards the spirit dog with tail and hair raised high, hissing and swiping with claws out to chase him into the Light. The husky gave a playful bark, shoulders down and haunches high. At Fish's louder, more insistent yowl, the dog yipped once more and raced down the tunnel of light for his own personal paradise. The cat sat back on his haunches and gave his partner a long-suffering sigh.

"No dogs, either, I assume?" The Reaper sighed and pulled out her tablet once more.

"And no cats!" Dave cut in, stepping around the mortal remains of the dog. "No elephants, or birds, or beetles. Just regular *human* people. Men people. And maybe 24, 25, single, not too ugly?"

"Would you like to add 'millionaire' to the list while we're customizing?" Fish groused.

"Squabble later," Helen said, cutting off whatever retort Dave was about to make. "We're already behind schedule and I'm just as eager to be out of this mess as either of you."

"Well, well, well," Fish mused. "Someone has her robe in a twist. Lead the way. Let's see what Contestant Number 3 has to offer."

"Less hair, I hope," Dave remarked as he followed the pair into the shadows.

—◦—

The trio emerged onto the well-groomed yard of a slick, modern-designed mansion. Soft lights glowed beneath a lap pool, illuminating a slender robed figure hunched over a form along the pool's edge while a green and orange parrot walked in slow circles nearby.

"Hey, is that-" Fish abruptly ended the sentence in a *huff* as Helen scooped him up and practically threw herself behind a cluster of trimmed bushes. Dave scrambled to duck behind her, his perpetual look of bewilderment still plastered on his face but willing to follow a Reaper's lead without knowing why.

Fish pulled his head out of Helen's sleeve, tongue furiously flicking out bits of vile fuzz made of a hellish mix of burlap and wool. He twisted around to deliver an angry glare into the depths of Helen's gaping hood.

"You're poaching another Reaper's mark?" he hissed. Reapers stuck to their own list, always—no exceptions. To even consider reaping another's mark risked a duel. Those scythes weren't just for show. It was the only weapon across dimensions that could defeat a Reaper permanently. Do not collect $200, go directly to oblivion kind of defeat.

Helen *shhhd* for him to keep his voice down. "I don't want the Soul, I want the body."

Fish snapped his mouth shut and slid softly from Helen's arm, crouching beneath a gap in the bush to watch the scene.

The tall Reaper touched the body, the spirit of the dead man appearing at its side instantly. The tunnel opened several feet away and Fish watched jealously as the parrot herded the new spirit inside with no problem. No annoying questions, no whining or negotiating, just straight to business.

What he wouldn't give for such an easy assignment at least once. He bet that bird never had to worry about getting *his* feathers roasted because *his* Reaper couldn't tell a human on his deathbed from one just out for a stroll.

After the tunnel closed, the parrot perched on the Reaper's shoulder and the pair apparated into thin air. Fish trotted out to inspect the body abandoned on the patio. Helen glided after him, Dave practically tripping over her robes as he stumbled out from behind the bush.

The body seemed to be everything Dave had requested, and more. The man had been somewhere between 23 to 27 and, aside from being dead, appeared in peak condition. Sleek athletic build stuffed into tight swim trunks left little to the imagination, and while Fish was no judge of human attractiveness, he found nothing offensive in his features. No wounds oozed or bones protruded, skin still held a healthy glow. He looked like he might pop up any second, good as new. And if Helen did her job right, he'd do just that.

"Well, well, well," Fish crowed, circling the corpse. "Mid-twenties, obviously male, doesn't seem to have expired from any ghastly disease, and—if this house is anything to go by—not doing too badly in the financial department. Will this one satisfy your demands?"

Dave frowned, leaning over to scrutinize the corpse as close as he dared without invading some perceived notion of personal space. "I don't know." He hesitated, straightening. "It seems alright as long as there's not something wrong with it. What killed him?"

Helen raised a bony finger to her face-hole in contemplation. After a moment, she shrugged, splaying her skeletal hand out in ignorance. "Some accident, I think. But he doesn't appear to be damaged."

"Are you gonna hop in, or what? The night is wasting!"

Dave scratched his head, mulling it over for a moment before shaking his head and throwing his arms up in defeat. "Why the hell not? When am I going to get a chance like this again, right?"

"Never," Fish snorted. "The answer better be never. My eternal nerves can't handle another debacle like this again. Right, Helen?"

Helen swung the front of her cowl towards him and he bristled under the staring blackness. Was she smiling in there? Frowning? He needed to get her a dramatic mask if she insisted on staring at him so frequently.

"I don't make promises," she replied in that same even cant she always used. Fish couldn't even tell her mood from the tone of her voice. The next 277 years couldn't come fast enough.

"Never too late to start."

"Guys," Dave interrupted, gesturing to the near-forgotten body on the ground. "Can we get this over with, or what? I've spent enough time as a wandering ghost, thank you."

"Oh, of course, of course, Dave. We are here but to serve you." Fish dipped his head in a mock bow, brow whiskers tilted up in irritation. "All on your time, of course."

"And well you should," the spirit snapped back. "I'm not supposed to be dead in the first place!"

"Which will be rectified shortly," Helen soothed, sweeping between the pair before their argument could escalate further. "In you go, and then we can all be on our way."

Mollified, Fish sat back on his haunches, bringing a paw up for a few calming licks. For once, the Dodo-headed Reaper was right. Just a few moments more and this horror of a night would be over and forgotten.

Dave took his place at the head of the corpse. Helen moved to the feet, taking what Fish termed her Thinking Hard pose—back straight, scythe parallel to her spine, free arm reaching towards the target. Fish held his breath for a tense moment, afraid Helen would forget what she was doing again, or Dave would get cold feet at the last second. At this point, he wouldn't be surprised if an anvil fell from the sky to ruin a perfectly good body. Certainly wouldn't be the strangest thing he'd experienced since becoming a psychopomp.

No anvil fell, nor did Dave suddenly cut and run. A simple, almost delicate wave and flick of Helen's exposed phalanges and Dave's spirit *poofed*, immediately followed by the previously uninhabited body kicking and breathing again.

Well, kicking, at least. Dave seemed to be having trouble breathing in his new form. He stared at Helen, bug-eyed and purple-faced, arms flailing in a panic.

"Oh, by Persephone's fingers, what have you done now?" Fish demanding, trotting closer to examine the panicking Dave, now beating at his chest while he rocked back and forth like an overturned turtle.

Helen clicked her hand bones together in a gesture of triumph. "Drowning," she declared.

"What?"

"The accident," she clarified, tilting her head towards Fish and shrugging. She pointed at the body Dave was currently struggling to oxygenate. "He died by accidental drowning. I knew it was something."

"And now Dave's drowning?!" Fish couldn't keep the undignified screech out of his voice. He remembered his own demise and could very well sympathize with Dave at that exact moment. The hair along his spine rose, and he twisted in frantic circles as Dave's movements began to wan. "Pull him out, Helen! This isn't going to work! Pull him out!"

Reaching down, Helen touched the big toe of one jerking foot, and the body stilled. Dave appeared beside her, gasping for air between hoarse coughs, one hand pressed to his aching chest.

"I'm sorry, Dave. I forgot about the whole breathing thing," Helen said, resting a comforting hand on Dave's shoulder.

"You forgot?" He glared at her, shrugging the hand off and stepping away. "You know what, I give up. Dying twice is more than enough for me. Just open the damn tunnel and let me go. Whatever's waiting for me over there has got to be better than hanging around with you."

Helen turned away from the steaming spirit to whisper, "Does this make it the tenth time?"

Fish flattened his ears in disbelief, eyes narrowing. You'd think Reapers would be required to pass a basic sensitivity course before taking up the hood.

"I don't think that one counts, Helen. I think each Soul only counts as one, no matter how many times you kill him."

The Reaper straightened abruptly, shoulders drawn back in offense. "I didn't do it on purpose. There's too many rules to being alive. I only know the rules for being dead."

Closing his eyes, Fish took in a deep breath and let it out slowly. "You're right. Death is your job. And it's my job to help you understand the living. So, why don't we just start over. Okay, Dave? Let's all just start over."

Dave halted his pacing and grumbling, facing Fish with arms folded and jaw set tense.

"No. I've had enough. I mean, what's next, a burn victim? A tragic parasailing accident? No, thank you. That creature couldn't pick a good body if it was handed to her on a silver platter!"

Fish ignored the flailing theatrics and focused on keeping Dave on this side of the Veil. If he insisted Helen open a tunnel for him, their mistake would be discovered and existence as he knew it would be over.

"You are absolutely correct. Sorry, Helen, but he has a point. So, why don't we start over? I mean, *all the way* over?"

Dave calmed, letting his arms drop as he considered the suggestion. The anger deflated out of him, but his expression remained wary as he took a few steps closer.

"What do you mean?"

His lips curled over his canines in feline glee. This was going to work. He finally knew exactly how to get them out of this mess.

"Trust me, this is going to be perfect," he assured the spirit. Glancing at Helen, he waved a paw at her voluminous sleeve. "Pull out your list."

———◇———

The trio stepped into the melee of a bustling hospital room. Too many people filled the small space, making too much noise and vying for elbow room. Fish squinted against the harsh glare of the fluorescent lighting and dashed along the wall to avoid the ghostly kicks of scrambling nurses.

In the center of the room, a heavily pregnant woman sat on the bed, knees pulled up high and shoulders rolled forward as she labored. Sweat and tears glistened on her strained face, reddened with exertion. Her partner held her hand, whispering encouragement and comfort as another contraction ripped a scream from her throat.

At her feet, the doctor did her best to coach the frightened mother as she assessed the baby's progress, while nursing staff flitted about with towels, implements, and various other preparations. At the door, pressed anxiously against the small window, family members awaited the new arrival with a mix of concern and excitement etched on their faces.

Dave pressed himself against the far wall, eyes darting from one activity to the next, his face a mask of confused bewilderment.

"What's going on?"

Fish could hear the tinge of unease in his voice and didn't blame him one bit. It was quite apparent the birth was not going well.

"A new life is being born," Helen replied, keeping her hood pointed towards the crowning infant. She took a step towards the bed. "But it will not linger long."

"What? No!" Dave dug his fingers into the Reaper's robe, holding her back. "You can't do that. It's just a baby."

Helen calmly pried his fingers from her robe with her free hand and patted his shoulder. "When it is time, Death comes, and there's nothing that can be done."

She turned back to the bed, taking another step forward as the doctor began gently guiding the infant into the world. Dave reached out to stop Helen again and Fish pushed him back with a hard lean on his leg.

"But you can stop it. That's what your powers are for," Dave argued. "If you took me before it was my time, then you can refuse to take someone, too."

"That's why you're still with us, Dave," Fish soothed, rubbing against Dave's legs with a loud purr. "Because it wasn't your time. You're here, wandering around instead of enjoying your Afterlife. But this isn't one of Helen's mistakes. It's tragic and horrifying and seems pointless, but that's what Death is sometimes."

The Reaper crossed the room, coming to stand next to the doctor cradling a too blue and silent baby. The doctor swiftly moved to the side, setting the baby down on a table to remove the umbilical cord from the infant's neck with the assistance of two nurses. Helen stretched a hand between them, delicately tapping the newborn on the head. When she turned back around to face Fish and Dave, the spirit of the child laid nestled in the crook of her arm.

Dave gave a strangled cry, and Fish reached out a paw to give his ankle a consoling pat.

"The body, the life that would never have been," Helen began, "it's there for you, Dave. If you want it."

"This is the best chance you're going to get," Fish said, staring up at the spirit with a slow blink. "We can't give you back the life you had, but you can build a new one. That couple—they want a child, and you want to live. A clean slate, the chance to pick a different path, or do the same thing all over again. It's up to you. What do you say?"

As he finished his speech, Fish realized it wasn't just fear of his own eternity that concerned him, but Dave's, too. The guy hadn't deserved to be plucked from his mortal coil right in the middle of his timeline, and he shouldn't be saddled with a millennium of Limbo for it. Sure, he *needed* to live for the sake of their skins, but he also *deserved* to live.

Dave hadn't been a hero, and maybe never would be. He hadn't invented any life-altering technology or contributed in any meaningful way to society, but he might if he'd kept living. Helen's mistake had robbed his future, the future he might have provided to others, and thus the particulars of his Afterlife. This was his chance to fulfill his destiny in the here and now, and the Hereafter.

Large green eyes pleading with Dave to accept his second chance, Fish waited for a reply with tense shoulders and a hopeful heart. Dave looked about the room as he considered, watching the parents becoming increasingly concerned as their son remained silent, the medical staff working furiously to revive the tiny, cold body on the table, and Helen making soft cooing noises at the infant spirit in her arm.

With a deep breath, Dave closed his eyes and nodded. "I'll do it."

The tension drained out of Fish in such a rush he nearly went limp. Rising to all fours, he circled around the spirit's feet, gently nudging him towards the table before he could change his mind. Dave stood as close to the body's head as he could get without the physical forms of the nurses cutting through him and gave a final nod to Helen. The Reaper nodded back and Dave's spirit blinked out of sight.

The body of the infant screamed to life, and the room released a collective sigh of relief. After one more examination to make sure the danger had passed, a nurse scooped the little bundle up and laid him gently in the waiting arms of his exhausted and relieved parents. Fish watched, smiling as wide as his whiskered cheeks would allow, as the couple fussed over the new life they had wrought.

"Goodbye, Dave. Live well."

"No, not Dave. Not anymore," Helen corrected, slowly rocking the gently sleeping spirit held close to her thin chest. "Dave is now only a shadow in the mind of this new life. Not quite a memory, yet still a part of his personality, somewhere."

Fish trotted to Helen's side, and the pair turned away from the heartwarming scene. A tunnel opened in the corner, ready to take the infant Soul across the Veil. The Reaper cooed at the infant spirit again, promising to deliver him to his beautiful Afterlife.

"Do you think he'll remember any of this? Of his life before?" Fish mused as they began the long journey through the portal.

Helen mused on it a moment before replying, "He'll probably always feel a little out of time, but he'll never quite know why."

"Well, maybe he'll be a little more cautious in dark alleyways with this life. He's already died twice."

"What is that saying humans have? Third time's the charm?" Helen chuckled.

Fish felt his hair bristle. He doubted she'd learned a thing from the night's adventure, and it was just as well. At least his eternity would never be dull.

A LITTLE PROBLEM

A pounding on my apartment door interrupted my reading. I considered ignoring it and returning to the engaging adventures of a boy wizard, but a quick glance at the clock changed my mind. Nothing good comes knocking on your door at 2 am, and nothing good usually equaled a paycheck for me. As a freelance monster hunter, most of my jobs came in the wee hours of the night. Still, I couldn't help the long-suffering sigh that escaped as I set my book aside in disappointment.

The woman on the other side of the door was as human as they come: average height and build, dull brown eyes and dull brown hair. A trembling traveled her body and her lips parted slightly in that familiar expression humans fell into when first looking upon an Aos Si. You'd think after twenty years in this dimension I'd be used to the fawning by now, but it never ceased to annoy. I might be a magical faerie knight, but I wasn't in it for the perks. Some things were just genetic.

"Are you Max Egan?"

"That's what it says on the sign." I gestured to the plaque nailed to the exterior brick. *Max Egan. Private Hunter. Your problem is no problem.*

I thought it was rather succinct, but prospective clients still asked the same questions.

Do you handle nuisance Fae? I think I have a boggart in my basement. No problem.

I may have a werewolf on my property. No problem.

I just discovered the weird statue I bought is a gargoyle. Do you deal in those? If it flies, shrieks, bites, or breathes fire, I can handle it.

"I represent O'Flannagan's Extravaganza Circus, and we have a little problem."

My fingers twitched with the urge to slam the door in her face. I was familiar with this circus—by reputation only, of course. I abhorred places like that. They operated on the exploitation of Grym creatures. Chimeras, unicorns, ogres, gargoyles, any breed of Grym monster kidnapped from my home dimension and paraded in front of ogling humans for five bucks a pop. It embodied the very thing I disliked most about humans: their disrespect for other forms of life.

My mind flashed to my quickly dwindling bank account. I hadn't had a case in weeks, and cash flow was becoming a problem. If I was going to keep myself in electricity and food, I would have to temper my personal ethics. With concentrated effort, I pried my fingers from the doorknob and gestured the woman inside.

She stepped into the room and took a long glance around my office-slash-apartment. She must not have been very impressed with my modern decor because she turned to me with a frown of suspicion.

"Are you full Aos Si?"

I couldn't help the dramatic roll of my eyes. Every single time with these questions. The constant disbelief from clients because I 'didn't look the part' was less than flattering.

If you're Fae, why do you have a computer? You have a lot of metal and plastic furniture for a nature Grym. I thought Faes liked organic materials. You have a cell phone? Is that a surround system? Aren't you a little buff to be a faerie?

Okay, that last one was a little flattering, but come on! Because obviously, all Fae are tree-dwelling, flower-eating hicks who marvel at the humans' advanced technology. Personally, I enjoyed modern music, books, and catching the odd episode of *I Dream of Jeannie*. I worked out three times a week and had a curated closet of choice duds. We weren't living in the Dark Ages anymore.

I raised a clenched fist, feeling the tingling heat in my veins as I called upon my magic. My hand began to glow, sparks arcing out in pale blue tendrils as the woman watched. I let the energy surge, fully formed ball lightning crackled around my fist and filling the room with an undulating glow. The overhead light flickered and buzzed harshly, the modern electrical system disrupted by the electromagnetic field. The woman took a swift step back, her look of doubt now one of clear unease.

"That's enough. I believe you."

I dissipated the energy immediately, shaking my hand to rid it of the residual feeling of unused magic. Power called and not spent always left a sensation of being unfulfilled, a restlessness that urged you to run, fight, explode; anything for release. I shook my hand again, harder. It didn't help and I could feel the frustration rising.

"Do you have a job for me, or did you just come to stare at my pretty face?"

It came out harsher than I intended and the woman flinched, red flushing her cheeks. "Yes. We've had a bit of a problem with our zombie display. It's on the loose."

I groaned. Why did humans always insist on messing with things they couldn't control? Zombies were a plague, literally. One bite and before you knew it, one had multiplied into dozens. I hated them. The undead always gave me the willies.

"Your handler didn't kill it?" Every venue was required to have an ever-present handler in case something broke loose, a crisis-trained professional to protect the masses from their own stupidity.

She turned her face away from me, her voice tight when she spoke again. "He was killed. It happened during a show and there was a bit of a panic." She met my eyes again, and I caught a flash of guilt roll over her features. "We left. We all just left. Ran, actually."

I groaned, wiping a hand over my face. When would they learn to leave the dead in their graves? "Do you know where this shambler is now? I charge extra for tracking."

"Oh, it's still at the circus. Our magician put up wards so it can't escape. Look," she continued, voice once again brusque and businesslike, "it's already a massive PR nightmare. We're prepared to offer you five thousand in cash for eliminating the problem tonight."

I stared at the wad of green she pulled from her purse. It was enough to keep me in books and tacos for another couple of months. At five times the going rate for a single job, it was quite the extravagant offer, and she had to know how tempting it was. I should say no and let them find some other schmuck willing to tangle with the dead, but that was a lot of taco money.

"How many of them are there?" I pressed, sensing a catch.

She shrugged. "Just the one, last I knew."

Her statement didn't fill me with confidence. She wasn't telling me everything; it was a lot of money to off one zombie. However, I was desperate enough to risk a surprise or two for such a hefty payoff.

I reached for the cash. She pulled her hand back and jammed the money deep within the confines of her purse.

"Payment after. The job starts now. I'll take you in my car."

I raised my eyebrows at the swift maneuver but didn't argue. My terms of service were flexible, depending on the state of my finances.

"I'll get my gear."

The circus was situated on a barren stretch of land between the commercial district and the tract housing of suburban wonderland. Unlike a traditional circus, O'Flannagan's was a permanent structure comprising a concrete amphitheater painted in the classic red and white of the old traveling tents and an expansive parking lot. Banners of legendary creatures, digitally enhanced and printed in vibrant colors, hung from the domed roof with headings like "Acrobats with Real Wings", "The Deadly Chimera", "A Fire-Breathing Dragon". All of these would have been amazing to the average human, but toss in revealing costumes and well-timed pyrotechnics and I understood how O'Flannagan's could afford to offer me such a tempting fee. It was a place where the wonder never ceased and neither, I imagined, did the clamor for tickets.

The woman parked the car in front of the entrance door but didn't turn off the engine.

"I'll wait here. When you come out, you'll get your money."

I could hear the unspoken 'if' in her tone. She pulled something from between the seats and thrust it at me, a saucer-sized wooden disk engraved with a tree in a circle of stars. I could feel the energy emanating from it in a soft buzz that tickled at my senses.

"That's the Ward Key. It will allow you inside without letting anything else out. Don't let it get broken, or the ward will fail."

I was well-aware of how a Ward Key functioned, but it was the tenseness in her voice that had my eyebrows rising. Again, I had the feeling information was being withheld.

"There's just the one, right?"

Guilt washed over her face again. "Trust me, those who didn't make it out won't be getting back up again. There wasn't enough of them left."

I wanted to ask more questions, but the woman gestured for me to get out, her lips pressed together tightly. I shrugged. It didn't matter, anyway. One zombie or twenty, they'd all be dead by dawn.

I retrieved my broadsword from the backseat, slipping the leather harness over my shoulders so that the hilt protruded within easy grasp of my sword-hand. I had two other blades: a matched pair of stilettos strapped to my calves. That and my magic were the only weapons I'd need.

I stopped in front of the entry door, feeling the pushback of the warding. It wasn't particularly strong; any determined magician could break it. However, it wasn't designed to keep people out but the undead in.

Holding the Ward Key aloft, the hair on my arms stood on end as tremors rippled through the energy field. The air shimmered pale blue ever so slightly and I reached for the door handle. The door opened easily and I slipped inside, the ward snapping back in place as I crossed the threshold.

The interior was dim, bathed in the soft yellow glow of the emergency lights set at intervals along the wall. Flyers and spilled popcorn littered the hall, small articles of clothing and accessories left abandoned in what was obviously a mad panic for the door. The stench of blood assaulted me and I wrinkled my nose against it. My skin prickled with a sense of crushing oppression.

I was instantly on alert. A single undead in a facility accustomed to dealing with the aberrant shouldn't have a feeling of desperation to it. I wondered again just how bad their problem had become.

I moved down the entrance corridor, past the darkened displays of odd-shaped skeletons and photographic histories of O'Flannagan's Circus. Glass lay strewn on the floor beneath one case, splashes of blood on the sharp edges. A dark mass slumped against the wall, a tangle of limbs dressed in black with the word "STAFF" blazoned in white across the shirt. Mangled lumps of bloodied flesh and bone shards marked what had once been the head, suspiciously devoid of gooey brain matter. Above the body, a large bloody hole ringed in hair and other things I dared not identify spoke of a force the average zombie did not possess. The further down the hall I ventured, the more bodies that lay jumbled along the path mauled, crushed, and empty of brains.

The acidic tang of blood intensified as I rounded the corner, filling my sinuses with sweet, cloying death. I turned my head away from it, searching for a gulp of fresh air. I breathed deep and choked on the quick closure of my throat, bile rising in my mouth. Swallowing hard and closing my eyes, I forced my thoughts away from the horror my nose had already discovered.

When my stomach settled, I opened my eyes and looked out across the auditorium. I was prepared for what I would see, but that didn't stop the violent lurch of my innards as I gazed upon the mess their little zombie problem had made.

Bodies, or what was left of them, lay like broken dolls in aisles, across seats, on the soft sand that filled the performance ring. Crushed and bloodied, some with limbs ripped from joints, and all missing great portions of their heads. It was nothing like any zombie attack I had ever seen before.

In general, zombies were not polite eaters. There is always a level of visceral gore when undead creatures rip hands and teeth into living flesh. But these bodies were not gnawed and clawed. They were smashed, gouged, and crumpled like an angry toddler stomping through a flower bed.

Within the ring, more forms lay in unnatural heaps atop darkened patches of sand. Most of these were not human. A sprite, her species discernible only from the remnants of gossamer wings ground into the sand, lay trodden and headless, strips of flesh stretching out from the neck where her skull had been pulled from her shoulders. What remained of a glaistig sat crumpled in a heap, her antlers snapped and the cranium ripped open as if used as a giant wishbone. A werewolf, unicorn, and faun were tossed about in pieces, all reduced to tufts of fur and gore. My stomach roiled as a cold peel of sweat erupted over my skin.

A wet grunting turned my attention from the disturbing images to the far side of the ring. A gryphon lay prone on the floor. One wing had been torn from its socket, and the ribcage of the animal sunk in dramatically where the bones had been shattered. A hulking creature squatted over it, bald and grey-skinned, large fangs protruding from fat lips dripping thickly with blood and something much chunkier in consistency. One hand clutched a roughly carved club nearly as long as I was tall, the other scooped squishy brain matter from the gryphon's cracked skull and dribbled it hungrily into his waiting maw. A gaping hole oozed and festered just below the creature's ribcage, one eyelid flapping softly over an empty socket and a large chunk of flesh was missing from the left shoulder. I could sense the aura of death and decay that clung to the creature, the unmistakable taint of reanimated flesh. I slumped against the wall and cursed.

A little problem? There was nothing little about a nine foot tall club-wielding ogre with a bad case of the walking dead. I could tell from the lack of rot and the still limber movements of his fingers that the ogre had turned less than twelve hours ago. He was not the slow, atrophied shambler I had anticipated. He still retained the speed, strength and most of the thought processes he did in life. This was going to be more challenging than I had signed up for.

The only sure way to kill a zombie is to remove the head, and for that I was going to have to get closer than I wanted. Keeping low to the ground, I began a slow creep around the stadium. The zombie didn't look up from his meal, continuing his slow scooping and slurping. When the creature's back was in my line of view, I turned down an aisle and made my way towards the ring. My plan, the only sensible one when facing a zombie three feet taller and easily four times stronger, was to sneak up behind it and behead him before he realized I was there. In and out with all my limbs still attached. I had nearly reached the front row before my plan fell apart.

I sidestepped a particularly gruesome-looking body—directly into a puddle of half-congealed blood. My boot heel slid sideways sharply. I tore my attention from my target, but not in time to save my balance. With a sickening plop, I landed hard on my ass, one hand wrist-deep in the gaping cavity of the corpse beside me.

"Son of a bitch!"

I didn't dare look at my hand. Feeling the cold slickness was enough to send me into another fit of nausea. I closed my eyes, concentrating on my breathing and keeping my dinner where it belonged. Quickly, I yanked my hand from the ichor, the sensation sending a fit of the heebie-jeebies all over my body. When I opened my eyes again, it was to find the zombie staring directly at me, drawn away from his feeding at my outburst.

Shit. Guess an ambush was out.

I grabbed the back of a chair and pulled myself up. The zombie straightened, his mouth open and drool rolling out as he contemplated his next prey. I had no intention of adding my corpse to the throng. The element of surprise may have eluded me, but I was going to see what sheer balls could get me.

Pulling my sword from its sheath, I leaped over the short wall separating the chairs from the ring and charged. I hoped speed would trump strength and I could relieve the zombie of his head before he could do the same to me. The zombie watched me approach impassively, unable to feel the intimidation I usually relied upon to give myself an edge. Just as I raised my sword arm to strike, the zombie brought up his club, giving it a lazy swing which hit the blade with all the force of a cannonball.

The sword spun from my hand, landing in a spray of sand halfway across the ring. The force sent vibrations up my arm, my hand falling temporarily numb. If I had been holding the pommel any harder, my bones would have shattered. As it was, I had just enough time to tuck and roll to avoid the equally powerful backswing.

Weaponless and way too close to the business end of the massive club, I sprinted towards the first thing I saw. The thump of the zombie's heavy footfalls close behind me lent speed to my limbs as I grabbed the toeholds of the trapeze rig and climbed for the platform.

The pole shook and my hands slipped dangerously, nearly falling the fifteen or so feet I'd managed to climb. I glanced down to see the zombie growling up at me, huge hands wrapped around the pole and throttling it the way I've seen animals shake fruit from trees. I pulled a stiletto from its sheath, aiming for the creature's good eye. The zombie wavered as it peered up at me, just enough for my blade to miss its mark. Snarling at me with purpled lips, the zombie otherwise gave no indication it even registered the twelve-inch blade now protruding from his meaty right shoulder.

He stepped back, his rotting brain slowly turning over how best to dislodge me from my perch, and I took the opportunity to call on my magic. I closed my fist, summoning my power into a tight little ball that sparked and crackled with blue electricity. I had almost gathered enough to deliver a good zap when a resounding thwack and the violent shaking of the pole shattered my concentration. My foot slid off the grip and I clung desperately to the platform as the zombie bashed his club against the rigging again.

I didn't relish the likely outcome if the zombie succeeded in bringing the whole rig down. Flashes of my crumbled, headless body, the Zed lustfully sucking brain juice from my upturned cranium, seared my mind. I needed to find a way off the platform quickly. Down didn't look like an option, so I looked up. The trapeze bar was still on the hook. I might not be able to do any fancy tricks, but I hoped I could at least swing over to the other side.

Lifting the bar off the hook and gripping tight, I launched myself from the platform. My dismount was less than professional, but gravity and inertia provided me with the necessary speed to fly the distance. I didn't know the first thing about landing from a trapeze, so when I let go of the bar (a tad too early perhaps), I stumbled onto the platform with an awkward flailing. Latching onto the pole with both arms, I managed to stop myself from careening over the other side. When I had my feet firmly under me again, I paused to see how my determined opponent was faring.

The zombie had ceased his bashing when he realized I was no longer there. His one eye roamed over the heights above him before settling doggedly on me. It was that undead persistence that made them such a menace. The newly revived might not be very efficient, but damned if they weren't focused.

As he took a shuffling step in my direction, I knew I only had a couple of minutes to get down and formulate a winning strategy before Mr. Slightly Green turned me into Zombie Pâté.

With a quick glance across the ring below, I located my sword. It had landed a few yards from the body of the gryphon. Judging by the zombie's speed, which I calculated to be an almost casual meander, and the not-inconsiderable height of the platform, I was willing to bet I could reach the ground before he reached me. Then, it was just a quick dash to retrieve my blade and on to zombie-hacking followed by a hefty cash payout.

The trip down took longer than I anticipated, slowed by the slipping of my boots on the thin grips made for more nimble and bootless feet. My descent seemed to give the zombie a burst of speed, no doubt expecting his next meal. His casual meandering quickened to a loping amble. Panic rose as a crushing grip encircled my ankle and tugged.

I'm not going to make it!

Pain shot through my leg up to my hip and I let out a strained grunt, letting go of the handholds to spare my leg being wrenched from the socket. Sailing through the air, I landed abruptly on my back. My entire body, and seemingly the world around it, was jarred, bruised, and aching.

I groaned and forced my eyes open against the pain. The zombie was already hovering above me, weapon raised in the air. I rolled as he let his arm drop, a spray of sand brushing against my face as the club thumped into the spot my head had been not a second before. Somersaulting into a low crouch and twisting around on my knee, I thrust my hand towards the monster, a spark of fire arched from my fingertips. It was a handy trick all Aos Si possessed, a defensive magic that didn't need any concentration to emit, though the element released varied. The spark struck his pant leg, igniting the material in a burst of flame.

For reasons not yet fully explained by science, the undead were highly flammable and intensely afraid of fire. This zombie was no different. He stared at the growing flame with a single bulging eye, mouth hanging open, vocalizing his distress with something between a grunt and a scream. He dropped the club and stumbled away in a blind panic, big clumsy feet kicking up sand and arms flailing as if to wave the fire away.

I took advantage of his distraction to make a dash for my sword. Sprinting past him, I snatched the pommel from the sand. The relief I felt as I wrapped my fingers around the familiar grip chased away the panic of the past several minutes. I turned to my opponent one last time, confident.

The zombie still shuffled wildly, oblivious to his surroundings as he focused on getting away from the fire. I imagined the fear the creature must be feeling, the internal agony that drove the instinctual brain to run, the primal suffering of being unable to escape his flaming limbs. Ending his misery was the only humane thing to do.

Slicing at his Achilles' tendons, I brought the zombie down quickly. He fell face-first to the ground still moaning, grinding his face into the sand mindlessly. I braced one foot against his back and brought my blade down against the nape of his neck, intending to end it swiftly. Steel hit flesh, the edge lodging in the thick bone and cartilage of his spinal column. The zombie struggled in protest, but the head remained firmly attached. I yanked the blade out and tried again, and again. The sickening sound of bone cracking with each stroke, putrid blood oozing from the wound and assailing my nostrils, weakened my determination. The head *had* to be removed. It was the only sure way to know a zombie was dead for good, but all I wanted to do was puke out my guts and purge the sounds and smells from my head. It took three more strokes before the head softly rolled several inches away and I could finally let my arms drop to my side.

I took several steps back, breathing hard and trying not to look at the mess I had made. As my adrenaline slowed, the sights and smells seemed to intensify. Tangy, earthy gore mixed with the rancid stench of decayed blood overpowered me as I stumbled for the exit. My stomach twisted and that familiar cold chill erupted over my body as I bolted past stained seats and mangled forms, my boots sliding as I rounded the corner. The ward dropped—the key still on my person—as I burst from the entry door, taking in huge gulps of fresh night air to chase the lingering feel of death from my lungs. My pace slowed as I approached the still-waiting car, wanting to enjoy the cleansing crispness of life beyond the confines of the circus walls.

The woman stared at me with narrowed eyes as I approached, glancing over the bloody sword I still held in a limp grip, at the stains on my clothing. I reached into my pocket to retrieve the Ward Key, tossing it through the open window onto the passenger seat and leaned down, my elbow resting heavily on the door.

"Is it done?"

I looked at my sword, dripping thick, dark fluid, to my hand crusted to the wrist in substances I never wanted analyzed, thinking about all the shit I had just gone through and how badly I needed a scalding hot shower. Suddenly, I couldn't hold it anymore. My gut gave one final lurch and the contents of my stomach splashed across the leather-bound seat. The woman recoiled, horror plastered on her face. When the heaving subsided, I reached my gore-encrusted hand towards her. Her face twisted in disgust.

"Money," I demanded hoarsely, snapping my fingers.

She snatched her purse from the floorboard, rummaging for the cash and whimpering when hot stomach acid rolled down the strap to plop on her hand. She offered the wad of green with a trembling hand. I took the time to count it before stuffing it in my pocket. I straightened away from the car.

"Thanks. Think I'll walk back."

She turned back around in her seat, popping the gear into drive. I slapped my hand on the door to catch her attention, ducking my head into the car once again.

"Oh, and one more thing. If I ever hear of the circus making zombies out of anything ever again, you're going to have a problem with me."

The look on my face must have convinced her I was serious. She blanched, shivering, and nodded. I stepped back to let her leave. Wiping the blade as clean as was possible on my pant leg, I slid my sword back into its sheath and began the long walk home. My stiletto still protruded from the permanently dead ogre's shoulder, but I shrugged it off as a loss. No way I was going back to retrieve it.

After this little adventure, I was definitely raising my fees. Courage in the face of gross ickiness now double. I had survived my most cringe-worthy opponent yet, an abomination even among the undead. But I guess it was just all par for the course in the life of a freelance Grym.

I'm Max Egan, Monster Hunter. Your problem is no problem.

HAGGRAVATION

"D o you think Santa will bring me new boots this year?" Katie asked, peeling the faded pinafore from her thin frame as she readied for bed.

The pitiful fire sputtering in the small hearth did little to warm the small, poorly insulated room she shared with her brother. Katie shivered, her threadbare shift doing little to ward off the deep winter chill.

Peter helped Katie wiggle into a woolen nightgown, frowning at the way the fabric stretched over her shoulders and exposed her wrists. She would need new clothes all too soon. He was already tallying up how many hours of work it would take to replace her too-small dresses, wondering if he had enough time before the seams split.

"You're too old to believe in Santa, Kat," Peter said, tucking her under a patchwork quilt on one of two narrow cots practically filling the room. Those and a pair of ancient wardrobes were all the furniture the space could hold.

Katie pouted, eyes wide and glistening with the threat of tears. Peter sighed in defeat and reached out to wrap her in a warm, apologetic hug.

"I have a little money saved from my job. If Santa doesn't bring you new boots, I'll buy them for you," he promised.

Katie sniffed, pulling back with a shake of her head. "You can't spend your money on me, Peter. That's Santa's job. He promised he'd bring me boots when I told him what I wanted at the church dinner last week."

"You know that was only Mr. Harris dressed in a red suit, don't you, Kat?"

"No, it was Santa," Katie insisted, edging out from under her brother's arm. "I know he's real, and if you'd only have a little faith, I know he'd bring you something really nice. You have to believe in him, or Krampus comes and sticks you in his sack and beats you."

Peter laughed, remembering how he had once believed the childish tales himself. He didn't want to see his trusting sister disappointed Christmas morning when she opened her present and found just another of Mother's hand-knitted scarves instead of the new shoes she desperately needed but were too expensive for his parents to afford.

"Kat, you're eight years old. Surely, you realize by now-"

A loud thunk shook the rafters, raining paint chips and dust over their heads. They both looked up as something large and heavy skidded across the roof in a series of thumps and scrapes, eyes following the sound of movement along the length of the ceiling. Silence fell over the room for a tense moment, followed by the unmistakable crunch of shoes in the thick snow.

Katie's face lit up in delight. "Santa's come early!"

Tossing the quilt aside, she hopped off the bed and scurried over to the hearth. Crouching down and leaning as close to the flames as she dared without risking a burn, she twisted her face to peer up the flue in search of the familiar red suit.

A clump of snow fell down the chimney, hitting the burning logs with a soft sizzle, and Peter surged to his feet. Unease raced up his spine as he took a cautious step towards the hearth. Nothing which slunk around chimneys late at night could mean well. A whooshing sound roared in his ears as a powerful gust of air burst down the chimney. The flames winked out, leaving only the glint of moonlight off snow-covered roofs to illuminate the room. Katie rolled back from the hearth, coughing as ash swirled around her nose and mouth.

The ominous scraping of something sliding down the brick interior echoed through the shadowed room. Peter's skin prickled as his hair stood on end, practically strumming with the sudden energy that emanated from the chimney. He recognized that feeling. It was the feel of magic.

"That's not Santa," Peter warned, reaching down to pull Katie to her feet and away from the fireplace.

Grabbing the poker off the wall, he maneuvered himself between the now-dark fireplace and his sister. Katie pulled on his shoulder, pleading for a glimpse of Santa, but he kept her back with an outstretched arm. One fist tightly brandishing the thin rod before him, Peter trained his eyes on the open hearth and waited.

Big black boots appeared above the smoldering pile of wood, followed by twig-thin legs encased in red hose. A large red overcoat, so long it swirled around the booted heels, stretched across a bulging belly. As the body ducked under the low curve of the hearth to emerge into the room, Peter could almost believe Santa had indeed made a miraculous appearance. But the face that accompanied that jolly form was not friendly or jovial.

Stringy hair, white and dry as kindling, flanked a grey-skinned face scored by deep wrinkles and punctured by two black holes where eyes should be. The nose was long, protruding a full five inches from the prominent cheeks and ending in a sharp point above thin lips barely concealing a row of jagged, rotting teeth. Long-fingered hands bent at gnarled knuckles gripped a big black sack over one shoulder and dangled a long, odd-shaped club at the figure's side. Peter had never seen so hideous a creature.

Katie shrunk behind Peter, excitement withering into terror. "Krampus," she whispered shakily. "He's come for you. I told you he would."

Peter nudged her further back, planting himself firmly between his sister and the fearsome-looking intruder. He didn't believe in childish fairy tales—enough horror filled everyday life without imagining new ones—but the frightening character before him obviously did not hail from their world. He knew of the host of magical creatures that invaded their world from Grym, had even seen a pixie or two, but they preferred to stay to the woods and lakes away from populated areas. They weren't common in the cities, so Peter never suspected he'd ever have to go against one himself.

Mustering his courage, he raised the fire poker higher, muttering a prayer the beast was susceptible to iron like so many of its ilk.

"Thief! Filthy beast! Get out of my house," he demanded. "There's nothing for you here."

The intruder laughed, warbling and high-pitched. Peter made a threatening jab, hoping to scare his opponent away. The club swung up quickly, meeting the side of Peter's head with a muted thwack and he crumpled to the floor. Katie screamed, falling hard on her rump and scrambling back for the door, clawing at the handle blindly as she kept her eyes on the monster in front of her.

Her brother's body had barely touched the floor before the figure swung the black sack from its shoulder and brusquely rolled Peter inside. The latch finally released and Katie ran from the room, still screaming, as the intruder hefted the sack and disappeared up the chimney.

<hr>

By mid-morning on Christmas Eve, shoppers filled the streets with the last-minute bustle of holiday errands. At the office of *Kane and Hodges, Investigators of Oddities*, Cleopatra Kane peered over the edge of her morning newspaper to see the young girl still pacing in front of the window. Pedestrians laden with packages swerved around her as she shuffled first one direction, then the other, peeking longingly at the tinted glass with each turn.

Obviously, something deeply troubled the girl and Kane wondered when the child would muster the gall to open the door. The suspense chafed at her patience and she crossed her booted heels on the edge of the desk with a huff, tossing a long blonde braid over her shoulder.

Across the room, Perseus Hodge cleared his throat loudly, staring at her through gold-rimmed spectacles. "If you cannot show a modicum of decorum, at least show some respect for the furniture. You're getting mud on the ledger."

Kane rolled her eyes, setting her feet back on the floor with something less than grace. "It's near blank, anyway," Kane groused, rising from her chair and adjusting her vest with impatient little flicks.

The holiday season had been woefully bereft of cases (there hadn't been a good one since the Werewolf of Harwich), and Kane did not deal well with boredom. She strode to the window casing, absentmindedly twirling an etched pocket watch in her hands as she watched the nervous little girl fidget in the street.

Hodge knew that look. A warning glow of impish delight illuminated her features just before she did something which invariably cost them a lot of money and embarrassment. Not that they were lacking in the latter department. Professional hunters of the supernatural proved a difficult niche to succeed in, and Kane's proclivity for masculine attire combined with her eccentric and brusque personality did nothing to enhance their reputation.

Hodge grunted, turning back to his cataloging of malicious goblinkin by geological demographic. "You need a hobby to keep you busy instead of staring at loitering children indubitably up to no good."

"Such a cynic, Hodges. Poor little thing surely is in need of assistance."

Hodge sputtered a protest as Kane swung the door wide and coaxed the young girl inside. A closer perusal of the child did not change his opinion. Clad in split and frayed boots and a dress stained and mended one too many times over a frame quickly growing beyond the seams, she did not have the look of a paying client. Twisting dirty, calloused hands against her chest, the girl stared at them with wide, misty eyes puffy from prolonged pouts of crying. Hodge frowned and gave a shake of his ashen curls. At the very least, the girl had come to beg something of them.

"Good day, sir, um, ma'am. Detective?" she stuttered, taking in Kane's appearance in flustered gawking. A woman as tall and broad as most men, dressed in trousers and waistcoat, was an uncommon sight even in such a cosmopolitan city.

Kane smiled and leaned over, reaching out a friendly hand. "You can call me Detective Kane," she said, shaking the girl's small hand. "And this is Hodges."

"Professor Hodge."

Kane smiled, green eyes sparkling in mischief, and whispered to the girl, "It's a point of contention."

Hodge dropped his pen on the desk in frustration and stood. "My name is Professor Hodge, no S. There has never been an S, nor will there ever be, and I have earned the honorific Professor as a civilized and educated member of society. It is not a matter of debate." Having voiced his position, he turned to the fragile child and pinned her with his inquisitive glare. "What can we do for you?"

The girl took a step back and dipped into an awkward imitation of a curtsy. "How do you do? I'm Katie Pagett." Taking a deep breath, she rushed out, "My brother was kidnapped last night, and I need you to rescue him!"

"How atrocious," Kane breathed, interest piqued. "Do you know who took him?"

"Have you informed the police?" Hodge cut in. "Kidnappings really are a police concern."

Katie sniffed, glistening moisture welling in her eyes and spilling down her cheeks. "I tried to, but Mother won't let me. She doesn't believe me. But I saw Krampus take him."

Hodge blinked. "I'm sorry, what was that?"

Katie turned her earnest, tear-streaked face to him. "Last night, I saw Krampus come down the chimney and take Peter away."

Hodge scoffed, shuffling a couple of steps to lean against the edge of his desk, arms folded across his chest. He pinned the girl with a stern glare.

"Krampus? Red eyes, horns, the legs of a goat, covered in black fur? Are you sure it wasn't a burglar or someone wearing funny clothes?"

The little girl's face reddened, her fidgeting hands curling into fists of frustration.

"It didn't have horns, or the legs of a goat. And I don't think it was covered in fur. But it had to be him! I know it was," she insisted, stamping one worn sole on the floor. "I thought it was Santa, but it was just evil. It had a scary face and a big club and there wasn't any presents."

Kane knelt and wrapped her arms around the girl, muttering soft words to calm her. She braced her chin on top of the girl's head, glaring at Hodge.

"What is wrong with you, Hodges? Can't you see how upset she is? She's frightened and needs our help."

"Oh, now, really," Hodge began, rolling his eyes towards the ceiling and lifting his shoulders in an exaggerated shrug. "Do you expect me to believe a demon popped down her chimney and absconded with her brother? The story of Krampus is just to scare children into behaving. He's not real. Whatever happened to her brother has a logical explanation. Magical, maybe, but not Santa's evil twin. Likely, he just ran away. How old is your brother?"

"Fifteen," Katie choked.

"See? He probably decided to strike out on his own and didn't want your parents to know about it."

"Peter wouldn't do that," Katie retorted, thrusting her chin towards the dismissive scholar. "He loves me. He takes care of me. He works hard so we can have food. And now he's gone, and we owe so much rent. Without Peter home to help, we'll be kicked out in the snow."

"We'll look into it," Kane promised, guiding Katie to a chair and pouring her a cup of hot tea from the corner stove. To Hodge, she continued, "It's obvious *something* has happened to her brother."

Hodge screwed up his nose but relented. "Alright. It's probably just an angry house boggart, or something. We can take the case for a quid, as retainer."

Katie choked on her tea at the demand, lower lip trembling as tears threatened to fall once more. Kane patted her head comfortingly and smiled warmly. "We'll take the case. We can let the retainer slide just this once." Tossing an exasperated look at her partner, she continued, "Where is your holiday spirit?"

"The same place as our incoming accounts: absent."

He met her expectant gaze with stony resistance, willing the direness of their financial situation to override her generosity. Kane allowed the silent battle to wage a moment longer before her eyebrows arched in warning and he sighed.

Hodge pushed away from the desk, returning to his seat and his ledger. "Fine, we'll take the case. You'll do as you please, regardless of my advice."

Kane rewarded him with a toothy grin. "Never any doubt," she chirped.

Perching on the edge of her desk, leaning heavily on an elbow propped on her knee, she gave Katie her undivided attention. "Now, tell me exactly what happened."

———◆———

Mrs. Pagett frowned to find the two investigators on her front step an hour later. She didn't like trouble, and the tall woman in trousers and her dour partner looked like trouble, especially as the gentleman carried an expensive-looking leather case in one hand. Behind the woman, her daughter Katie peered up at her with a sheepish smile. Mrs. Pagett glowered back.

"Hello, Mrs. Pagett," Kane greeted, sweeping her bowler hat from her head. "I'm Detective Kane, and this is Hodges. We're investigating the disappearance of your son, Peter. May we come inside?"

"Professor Hodge, Mrs. Pagett. No S. How do you do?" Hodge greeted, extending a friendly hand.

Mrs. Pagett ignored the hand, her own tightening on the handle of the door as she considered whether to slam it in their faces. After a silent moment, she released a huff and stood aside, gesturing for the unwelcome visitors to enter.

Kane stepped into the parlor, scanning a keen eye about the quarters. The small home felt cramped—the fire too low and the windows too drafty—though clean and well-appointed. Old but carefully maintained furniture squatted about the room, with a smattering of seasonal decorations here and there. A pair of faded Christmas stockings embroidered with the Pagett children's names hung from the mantel, partially filled with meager offerings of rock candy and trinkets.

"Peter isn't missing," Mrs. Pagett said once Hodge had closed the door against the winter chill. "He's run off, and that's about the end of it. Katie had no business involving you."

Katie blushed brightly at her mother's words, bowing her head in a gesture of apology.

Kane cocked her head to the side, watching Mrs. Pagett carefully. "I understand that would be uncharacteristic of Peter. Are you sure he left of his own free will?"

The older woman shrugged, focusing on rubbing imagined dirt from her palms with the dingy apron that covered her gown. Her voice quavered, tears lurking just behind the hard exterior.

"He's of age to strike out on his own. Not much holding him here. He works at the shop on Dean Street, but he'd make quite a bit more in the Navy or out West."

Hodge gave Kane his best I-told-you-so grin, tapping his empty hand against his thigh to signal he felt the investigation over and they should leave. Kane ignored him.

"Had Peter mentioned wishing to leave?"

"No," Mrs. Pagett admitted, her lips twisting up in a half-hearted smile. "But sons don't always confide in mothers."

Spreading her arms in an encompassing gesture, Kane pressed, "But to leave at Yuletide? Two days before Christmas? A bit unusual, isn't it?"

Mrs. Pagett glanced away, huffing for something to say but not coming up with anything to adequately explain the timing of her son's disappearance. Kane took a step closer and pressed on.

"Katie reported a fellow of some sort in her room. Came down the chimney. Nothing peculiar occurred last night that you noticed? No odd sounds? And you didn't see Peter leave?"

The woman hesitated again, guilt playing across her eyes. The look quickly disappeared, stubbornness setting her jaw. She puffed her chest out, tone defensive.

"There were noises. Might have been the roof. Might as not. I mind my own business, especially after dark. Where my son comes and goes is his own concern. He's grown enough."

Kane bit down on her lips to keep from snapping at the woman. Mrs. Pagett's lack of cooperation and concern for her child grew increasingly frustrating, threatening to stoke the detective's ire. She took a step back, gesturing around the room with a wave of her hat.

"Mind if we take a look around?"

Mrs. Pagett nodded and Katie led the pair up the narrow stairs to the small room she shared with her brother. The room had a cramped feel, two narrow beds flanking a hearth and a pair of crooked wardrobes against one wall holding all of the sibling's possessions. A draft swirled around the room, making it feel more chill than it should, the fire long since extinguished. Sooty footprints circled the hearth.

"Did you show your mother these?" Kane asked, squatting for a closer look.

Katie nodded. "She said I made them to scare her."

The prints left behind were certainly not that of a hooved creature like Krampus, nor were they the dainty shape of a little girl. Letting her eyes follow the line of the prints to the hearth, Kane spotted a wisp of long white hair wafting in the draft on the edge of the bricks. Plucking the stray strand from the wall, she ran it through her hands, feeling its coarseness. She brought it to her nose for a quick sniff, nostrils burning with the telltale aroma of magic.

Hodge appeared at her side, leaning under the corner of the mantel to peer up into the darkness.

"Well, whatever made those footprints had to be a rather small fellow. Can't imagine they'd have been able to pull a young man up this chimney, though."

"Oh, no," Katie corrected. "It wasn't very tall, but it had a great big belly and strong arms. Knocked Peter right out and carried him away."

"Preposterous," Hodge replied, measuring the width of the flue with his palm. "*You'd* barely fit up there, let alone an abductor with a near-grown boy on his back."

Kane frowned, brushing the hair from her hand, and strode towards the small window. Kneeling across one of the narrow cots, she pushed the pane up and she stuck her head out to gauge the route to the roof.

Deeming it an easy enough distance, Kane turned and picked up the leather case Hodge had set down just inside the door. Dropping it on the cot, she flicked it open and rummaged through the contents. Pulling a pair of goggles sprouting with knobs and switches from the case, she turned to Hodge, who had abandoned his inspection of the hearth and now stood beside her.

"Shall we?" She smiled, gesturing to the window with a jerk of her head.

"Shall we what? On the roof?" Hodge asked incredulously. He shook his head, holding his hands up to wave away the suggestion. "No, no. I'm better suited to the ground, thank you."

"Suit yourself." Kane shrugged, sliding the awkward-looking goggles over her head.

"What are those for?" Katie asked, pointing to the grey-tinted and multi-lensed eyewear.

"They help me see things that aren't really there."

At her puzzled look, Hodge clarified, "Things not of this natural earth—fairies, ghouls, werewolves, witches, things from the Grym world—leave behind a trail. A magic residue, so to speak. Those goggles make them visible to the wearer."

Katie crossed her arms over her thin chest, one foot outward, and pinned Hodge with a derisive stare. "You believe in fairies and werewolves but not Krampus?"

Hodge mirrored her stance, his lip curling up in a mocking manner. "I've never *seen* a Krampus."

Kane shoved the case in Hodges' hands, interrupting the childish display. She knelt across the cot once more, shoving the curtains out of the way.

"I found a white hair stuck to the fireplace, rotten with magic. Krampus is said to be black as pitch, so it couldn't be that demon. However, it's not a common thief, either," she announced, sticking one leg out the window. "Maybe whatever it left behind at the entry point will give me a clue."

Hodge leaned over the cot as she slipped out the window, cautiously peering out to judge the distance to the ground below. "If you fall, you can hobble yourself to the hospital."

Kane smiled, not in the least concerned. "I scaled the clock tower hunting down a harpy that escaped from the circus without so much as a grappling hook. I'll be fine."

Balancing precariously on the ledge, Kane bent slightly and launched herself towards the rounded gutter that ran just under the eaves. In a feat of upper body strength and acrobatics Hodge had not known her capable of, Kane was navigating the snow-slicked surface of the roof in moments.

The deep imprints along the middle of the roof were immediately apparent. Not the marks of a sleigh and reindeer sliding across the surface, but rather something large and round skipping like a boulder. The circular depressions were almost a meter wide, split by a thin trail of ice where the snow had been flash-melted and refrozen. Where the deep impressions ended, boot prints began, leading to the chimney and crossing over again on the journey back. The second set of prints were deeper, made by a creature much heavier on its return voyage—likely from the added burden of Peter.

Kane reached up and flicked a switch just to the side of the right lens, the goggles powering on with a soft hum and a flash of light across the magic-tempered glass. Adjusting a knob to account for the brightness of day, Kane scanned her vision over the roof. A pulsating streak of purple infused with green cut over the bright snow in a superimposed glow. At the end of the trail, the green branched off, snaking down the chimney.

Kane strode over to the opening of the chimney stack and peered down. It was indeed too narrow for a young man like Peter to fit through with ease, much less two people. But the flood of green light that filled the space from brick to brick explained how such a thing could be accomplished.

Of all the aura colors left behind by the inhabitants of the Grym, Kane liked green the least. There were many creatures which used magic to perform mischief, but none were as difficult to deal with as Hags. As shape-changers, they shifted form at will and possessed a strength far greater than their size suggested. To make matters worse, they commanded an arsenal of magics that made them formidable opponents to even well-versed sorcerers.

Soulless, twisted creatures with a taste for human flesh, Kane would much preferred to have dealt with an actual demon than a Hag. Demons, at least, were bound by rules and limitations. Hags had no such constraints, and their only goal in life seemed to be terrorizing the populace.

Kane glanced around the rooftops, looking for more signs of the Hag's presence. The purple trail—evidence of a magical device in use—continued from the Pagett home along an intermittent path weaving from one roof to the next. The device didn't seem to take actual flight if the clear trail was any indication, which would make it easier to track.

Kane agilely climbed back inside the room, flicking off the goggles and tossing them to Hodge.

"Well?" Hodge asked expectantly as he carefully folded the goggles back into their place.

Kane ignored him, not quite prepared to tell him what they were up against. He would take the news much better down on the street, where his reaction would be tempered by his desire to avoid a public scene.

She turned to Katie and placed a reassuring hand on the young girl's shoulder. "We'll get your brother back." It was a promise she intended to keep.

Politely saying their farewells to Mrs. Pagett and her daughter, Kane and Hodge stepped out into the slush-filled lane. Hodge climbed into Kane's custom-built Motorwagen and cranked the engine to life, his partner hopping into the seat beside him.

"You might as well come out with it," Hodge began, clicking the long stick shift into gear and letting the contraption slowly roll away from the curb, people scurrying quickly out of the way at the sight of the motorized carriage. "I'm going to find out what we're dealing with sooner or later. Best to be prepared ahead of time."

Kane grimaced, already imagining Hodge's disapproval. "What do you recall of Hags?"

"Oh, no," Hodge groaned, letting his forehead rest on the steering wheel briefly in defeat. "We in no way possess the expertise to tangle with Hags. This has gone way beyond us already. I wouldn't even know how to track the bloody thing."

"That shouldn't be too hard," Kane replied. "It left a trail all over town."

"That doesn't solve the problem of what we do with it once we find it."

Kane shrugged, not overly concerned with the planning aspect of their job. "Hit it with whatever we've got until it surrenders, I suppose."

Hodge glanced at her, lips pressed tight and eyebrows quirked in a dubious expression. "That doesn't sound like a very effective plan, Kane. We really need to look into these creatures before we barge right in."

"Hags have a habit of eating their victims, Hodge," she reminded him curtly. "Peter doesn't have time for us to fiddle around with research."

"Right, so, take everything we've got and hope for the best. As usual." He grumbled a curse under his breath. "I hate my job."

Kane smiled, not at all put off by Hodge's defeatist attitude. She nudged him with her shoulder and teased, "You love it and you know it. Chasing off vampires, banishing poltergeists, capturing creatures of pure nightmare. It's titillating."

"The fear, the adrenaline, the apoplexy," he groused. "What I wouldn't give for something a little more boring."

"Now, what would be the fun in that?"

Hodge sighed. What Kane found exciting he considered unnecessary risks. And tonight promised to be yet another venture they'd be lucky to get out of alive.

———◦◇◦———

Back at the office, the pair wasted no time preparing as much as they could for their rescue mission. Unsure exactly what might harm a Hag, Kane armed herself with a wide-ranging arsenal of weapons. She slid a runic-inscribed hunting knife into the top of her boot, tucked a rifle loaded with silver bullets under her arm, and slung a net cannon across her back. Just for good measure, she belted a satchel of vials and potions commissioned from the local Hedgewitch to cover a host of situations around her waist. Hodge, not as well versed in combat as Kane, carried only a collection of homemade alchemy grenades, a revolving pistol, and a portable trunk filled with various paranormal defense concoctions and relics over his shoulder.

"Did you find anything useful?" Kane asked as Hodge rejoined her at the Motorwagen, his Encyclopedia of Vile Creatures clutched in one hand.

He shook his head, tossing his gear in the back and climbing into the driver's seat. "Nothing on Hags that isn't simply fairy tale nonsense. We'll have to guess our way to victory. Again."

"That just makes it more exciting."

⸺◇⸺

Hodge steered the carriage back to the Pagett house and the start of the trail. Sliding her aura-detecting goggles back on, Kane directed Hodge along the meandering path of the purple trail. Aura trails did not last forever, and this one was already beginning to fade. They had to back-track several times to pick up the path in the winding streets.

The rows of quaint shops and narrow houses were slowly replaced by leaning warehouses and crumbling factories. The thinning trail ended at the entrance of an abandoned fish processing plant. Kane leapt down from the seat, adjusted the weight of the net cannon on her back and started towards the heavy wooden doors. Hodge scrambled to her side, placing a restraining hand on her shoulder.

"Wards," he warned, pointing to the ground.

Kane looked down to see a swath of snow swept away in a line encircling the building. A line of archaic runes were etched in the exposed dirt, creating a protective barrier around the property. The moment they crossed the line, the Hag would be alerted to their presence. Kane frowned at the added complication.

"We can't set off the wards too early and lose our edge of surprise. How do you want to handle this?" Hodge asked.

"The same way I handle everything," Kane answered, shaking off his hand and striding straight for the front door. Hodge cursed and rushed to grab his kit from the vehicle, trotting awkwardly to catch up to his impulsive partner. He darted his eyes this way and that, covering Kane's back from any potential ambush. She didn't seem to share his concern.

Kane tried the handle of the door, not surprised to find it unlocked. Magical protections and wards made average locks completely unnecessary. Most casual trespassers weren't likely to survive for long after entering uninvited.

Sunlight filtering through gaps in the wall and ceiling lit the interior of the plant in a dim, dust-filled haze. Pieces of machinery lay scattered about the factory floor, the vague scent of rot and rat droppings filling the musty air. The center of the room had been cleared of debris and in that space sat a two-storey house, looking like a child's clubhouse inside the much larger structure. A barrel-shaped cart sat on the front door next to a long, club-shaped object leaning against the jamb, wind chimes and dried herbs hanging from the low awning.

Built in a quaint cottage-style with a thatched roof, the white-washed walls and faded red trim would have been perfect in the wooded countryside. Here, in the shadows of an abandoned fish factory, its presence took on a more ominous feel.

Shadows of movement crossed the flickering light shining from the front windows. Kane ducked behind a pile of broken wood just as the cottage door opened, Hodge falling to his knees beside her. Three figures emerged, each one a fearsome, wizened Hag. The first one to appear wore all red, the description matching the creature Katie saw take Peter. Behind it came a squatter, rounder version in patchwork clothing, followed by a lanky, thin creature in blue robes. All three had their pointy noses to the air sniffing furiously, and all three glowed bright green in the lens of Kane's goggles.

"Oh, Lord, there's three of them," Hodge groaned, rolling back on his haunches to lean against the wood. He closed his eyes and murmured a quick prayer of protection before carefully sliding his pack off his back to quietly rummage through the contents in search of a useful weapon.

"I smell intruders. Yagi! Go find out who that is," the red-clad Hag yelled, gesturing in the general direction of Kane and Hodge's hiding place.

"Not my turn," the lanky one whined. "Send Yagoi."

"Yaga should go," the third replied. "She has a nose for such things."

Yaga moved with a speed such an old and round body should not have been capable of. Raising a gnarled hand, she struck first one and then the other of her companions, leaving behind thin red marks where her nails sliced their skin.

"Younger sisters do as they're told. I will tend the soup," Yaga announced, stomping back into the cottage.

The round Yagoi sniffed derisively at her thinner sister and turned to follow Yaga back inside. The tall Yagi, grumbling something under her breath, marched towards the door, scanning the shadowed crevices of the debris as she went.

"What have you got, Hodges?" Kane asked, snapping her fingers impatiently as she kept an eye on Yagi's progress. The Hag sniffed at the air every few feet, eyes peering sharply into the shadows, but she hadn't picked up their essence yet. Kane knew it wouldn't be long before the Hag sussed them out and they needed to be ready to strike first.

Hodge's voice rose an octave in his panic. "I don't know what to try." He dug through his small chest of artifacts with desperate fingers. "I've got Wolfsbane, garlic, mandrake root, a finger bone from Saint Peter, stakes. What do I do for Hag?"

"I don't know, but you have about fifteen seconds to figure it out."

Hodge fumbled with his bottles. "If we survive this, I'm going to need a raise."

The Hag had almost come abreast of them, now. Another couple of steps and they'd both be caught.

"I'll take that under consideration. Meanwhile, find something to rescue me before I get eaten," Kane replied, pushing up to her feet. Hodge turned to protest, but she had already stepped away from the pile of wood, rifle leveled at the approaching creature.

"No closer, if you please. I'm an excellent shot," Kane warned.

The Hag halted, studying Kane with her head tilted to one side, black marble eyes burning from behind a curtain of lank, grey hair. The Grym didn't seem to fear her, an emotion Kane had been banking on and whose lack greatly curtailed her plans. If she couldn't intimidate it, she wasn't sure she could stall it long enough for Hodge to do something useful.

"You have wandered into the wrong place," Yagi said, its voice as rough as a stone against sandpaper. "Nothing for you to do here but die."

Kane raised her eyebrows. She's heard that same line from a dozen monsters. "I'm inquiring about the disappearance of a young man named Peter Pagett. Sound familiar to you?"

Yagi rolled her head, either in a nod or contemplation Kane couldn't tell. "Many children here. I do not bother to learn their names. *Dinner* is all I call them."

"There's going to be a slight alteration to the menu tonight," Kane said, pulling the hammer back on her rifle.

"Well, if you're offering," Yagi began, reaching for the wide belt at her waist. "You're a bit old to be very tasty, but I suppose you'll do as a palate cleanser."

The Hag took another step closer, hand disappearing further into the reaches of its rags. Kane wasn't about to let it reach whatever it had hidden in the folds of its robe. She fired, the bullet ripping through the upper chest of the Hag in the soft spot between heart and shoulder.

Yagi took a half step back, staring at the hole in surprise. Black fluid stained the blue of the robe, but it had little effect otherwise. Narrowing its dark eyes at Kane, it screamed, the keening, high-pitched sound reverberating through the building. The sound pierced her brain like a knife and Kane lowered the rifle to press a hand to her ear, groaning against the agony that swelled in her head.

Her victim suitably distracted, Yagi pulled a whip from behind her long back and flicked its length around Kane's torso. The thick coils wrapped around the woman's middle tighter and tighter, slithering like a snake. Arms pinned close to her ribs, the rifle dropped to the ground as the sharp edges of the net cannon dug into her back painfully. Yagi snapped her mouth shut, ending the paralyzing effects of the keening.

"That was unexpected and not entirely fair," Kane protested as Yagi tugged hard on the whip. She hopped forward awkwardly to avoid toppling to the ground. Lying prone seemed like an even worse predicament than what she was already in.

Yagi gave a short bark of laughter and pulled on the tether, forcing Kane to follow it towards the cottage. Twisting her head to look back at

Hodge still watching the scene from behind the woodpile, she gave him a poignant look, hoping he had something to use against the Hags. He merely shook his head and lifted his arms in a shrug. Rolling her eyes, she mumbled something about scholars being useless and turned back around.

"What?" Yagi turned on its heel, peering intently at the piles of debris around the door. Kane scooted into her line of sight, blocking it from catching a glimpse—or whiff—of Hodge.

"Where are we going?" Kane asked innocently, keeping the Hag's attention on herself. If Hodge got spotted now, neither of them would escape.

Yagi slowly rotated back around, giving the tether a tug to get Kane moving again. "To my sisters. Yaga will decide how best to be rid of you."

The myriad of ways that could be employed to end her life didn't bear thinking about. She needed a delaying tactic, something—*anything*—to give Hodge more time to form some kind of plan. Flexing her arms experimentally, the enchanted whip tightened around her further, threatening to restrict her breathing. Wiggling free didn't appear to be an option.

Reaching the cottage door, Yagi yanked her captive inside. The single room appeared smaller than Kane would have suspected, each corner taken up by a large metal coil, the function of which she couldn't begin to guess. Rough-hewn furniture divided the space into a kitchen, dining room, and sitting room. A couch cushioned with scraps of rugs lay near the door, flanked by an end table topped with a scattering of leather-bound books. Towards the back of the house sat a poorly constructed dining table and three chairs, knots of wood scarring the uneven surface. To Kane's left, a large black pot bubbling over an open fire pit which dominated the kitchen area. The other two Hags stood bent over this pot, stirring in dried herbs and all manner of unsavory-looking chunks.

Along the wall between the living area and the dining table stretched a large iron cage, bolted in place and filled with crying children. Boys and girls of various ages and from all classes sat or stood huddled against the bars, dread paling their cheeks as they watched the Hags prepare the boiling stew. One stood taller than the rest, his face sullen and calm, arm wrapped protectively around a small, dark-haired girl no more than six.

"Oh, what did you find? What did you catch?" Yaga cooed, circling Kane as they stepped past the threshold. The Hag sniffed at her hair, along her neck, and poking the tip at her clothes, taking in deep whiffs. Kane recoiled as far as the whip would allow her.

"A firstborn. An only born. So sweet," it announced, rubbing its hands in glee and staring at Kane with hungry eyes.

"It's too old," the large Yagoi complained, jutting her pointed chin out with a derisive sniff. "The meat will be tough."

"It will be sweet," Yaga corrected. "Firstborns are always sweet. All their parents' hopes and dreams are imbued in their flesh. Succulent with essence. We'll put it in the pot."

Kane did not feel at all enthused at the suggestion she go in the pot. Hoping to keep them talking and distracted from completing their task, she gestured towards the children with her shoulder.

"Why do you have so many children here? There must be more than a dozen. Peter? Peter Pagett, is that you?" Kane asked of the tall boy, picking him out as the only one among the captives older than 10 rather than any resemblance to his sister.

In answer, Peter let go of the slight girl and pressed his face against the bars. A flicker of hope sparked in his eyes before being snuffed out again by the sight of their guards attentively watching their every move.

Yagi dropped the whip, distracted by children pressed against the bars, and Kane felt the leather loosen. She began to wiggle her shoulders, inching the coils down ever so slightly, mindful of the three Hags keeping an eye on her.

Walking over to the cage, Yagi scraped it's long nails against the iron, the children retreating back the far wall in a scramble. Only Peter remained stalwartly within reach, glaring at the Hag in defiance.

"It is our Yule feast. We celebrate the happiest time of the year by eating what parents hold most dear."

The Hag reached out, flicking the tip of a nail sharply over Peter's exposed forearm, the boy wincing as a thin red line appeared. Yagi raised the blood-tipped nail to her mouth and slowly licked the blood from the point with a sharp purple tongue.

"I'm afraid I can't let you do that," Kane said, shaking the whip free from her arms.

Swinging the net cannon around from behind her back, she aimed and fired directly at Yagi. The net ejected from the cannon and wrapped securely around the creature, dragging the screeching Hag to the floor.

The angry protestations of the sisters were interrupted in a shower of wooden shrapnel as something large and round crashed through the door of the cottage. Kane leapt out of the way, landing heavily on one hip. The contraption careened straight into the round Yagoi, pinning the Hag against the rough dining table and smashing both of them into the far wall in an explosion of wooden fragments and dark, sticky fluid.

Pushing herself from the floor as the dust settled, Kane surveyed the damage. A line of indents cut a path into the floorboards in the same pattern as those from the Pagett roof. Hodge emerged from inside the barrel-shaped cart, one hand clutching what had initially looked to be a club but Kane now saw to be a portable propulsion rocket.

"I found something that works!" Hodge stated triumphantly, brandishing the magical club overhead.

Yaga turned purple with rage at seeing her sister-Hag squished against the wall like a fly. Pulling a rock from her waist pouch, she began chanting ominously. Across the room, Yagi tore at the net with blade-sharp nails, shredding the rope as easily as if it were made of spiderweb.

"Angry Hags!" Kane warned, bracing herself and looking around for anything useful. "Do something again, Hodge!"

Determining the chanting Yaga to be the more imminent threat, Hodge aimed the propulsion rocket at the Hag and fired. The force blew

Hodge back against the ooze-covered wall, his head snapping backwards with stunning force. The blast end shot out a stream of super-powered air, hitting the side of the pot with enough force to tip it over on top of Yaga. The Hag screamed, convulsing in intense pain as boiling hot broth and heavy iron rolled over her body, her thin arms flailing uselessly at the heated metal. In seconds, the Hag had shriveled into a silent, foul-smelling mass. Awash with broth, tinted black from the blood of the melted Yaga, flowed over the floor and splashed up against Kane's boots. Grimacing, she tried not to think about the stain that would leave in the leather.

Across the room, Yagi had torn free of the net and Kane turned her focus to the snarling creature. Her one shot already spent, she held the cannon in front of her as a shield against the slashing of Yagi's clawed fingers. Ramming the barrel of the cannon into Yagi's midsection, she was satisfied to see the Hag doubled over from the force of the blow and Kane took a moment to regroup before it surged at her again.

"I can't hold it back for long, Hodge," Kane called, barely keeping the nails from reaching her face.

Hodge shook the disorientation from his head and struggled into a standing position. Sticky, viscous fluid covered his clothes, and he gagged at the feel of Hag-goo on his skin. Taking a step towards the tussling pair, he reached in his pocket and lobbed the first thing he grabbed. A small glass container holding a yellowed, rod-shaped object flew at the creature, only to be swatted away with the wave of a claw to shatter across the floor, ineffective.

"Ah, my reliquary," Hodge protested, watching helplessly as Saint Peter's purported finger skittered across the floor. He had paid good money for that sacred item, and it hadn't even given the Hag pause.

Plucking a smoke grenade from his belt, Hodge pulled the tab and hurled it at the Yagi, hoping it would at least distract the creature long enough for Kane to get the upper hand.

It bounced along the uneven boards, rolling to a stop between their shuffling feet. A thick plume of acidic smoke poured from the top of the grenade, stinging the eyes of the Hag. It stepped back, coughing and covering its face. Her own eyes still protected by her goggles, Kane pulled a handkerchief from her pocket and pressed it against her nose to prevent the burning gas from reaching her throat.

Hodge took up the propulsion staff again and charged the fumbling figure of the Hag, bringing the heavy, flared end down on its head. Stunned, Yagi slumped against the wall. Taking advantage of its weakened state, Kane pulled her hunting knife from her belt and drove it into the creature's heart, twisting and sawing in every direction until Yagi ceased to struggle and fell limp.

Exhaustion filled her limbs as the adrenaline subsided and Kane collapsed onto the couch. Hodge stumbled over and let his body fall next to her, sighing heavily from injury and fatigue, clothes covered in dark splotches that no amount of scrubbing would ever get out.

"That was a piece of cake," Kane said between breaths.

"You know, it actually was," Hodge agreed, huffing tiredly between pauses. "A nasty. Man-eating. Ugly as sin. Cake."

They looked at each other and smiled. Hodge reached up to brush a curl from his brow, his fingers coming away smeared with black ooze. He wiped the offending ichor on a clean spot of pant leg with a grimace.

Feeling the weight of 16 frightened and tired children staring at her, Kane pushed up from the couch, reaching out a hand to pull Hodge to his feet.

"So, how do we get all these young 'uns home?" she asked, grabbing the ring of keys from the hook near the cage and opening the door. The newly freed children filed out, cautiously stepping around the remnants of Hag bits that littered the floor.

"The house walks," one of the children offered.

"What?"

"The house walks. Under the cupboard, they've got a gearbox, and it makes the house walk. That's how it got in here in the first place," the child explained.

He pointed to what looked like a cabinet set beneath the large kitchen window. Kane strode over, pushing away Yagi's corpse with her boot to search inside. The door folded open, revealing several dials, cranks, buttons, and three levers marked in a language Kane recognized but possessed no skill in.

"How's your Grymmish, Hodges?"

Hodge leaned over, peering at the faded red writing above each knob and dial. He pushed up on the rim of his spectacles with one finger, squinting in concentration. "It's an older dialect, not so easy to translate.

If I'm reading it correctly, this one basically means 'Push to start'. The first lever-"

"That's all I need to know," Kane stated, punching down the 'start' button. The buttons began to glow with a bluish light and the electric sizzle of magic hummed through the house. The sound of an engine whirling to life filled the small cottage, the crockery on the shelves rattling.

"But there's a dozen other buttons and levers," Hodge protested, gesturing to the cluttered and complicated-looking control panel.

"I'll figure it out along the way." She glanced at the selection of knobs and dials, wondering which to try next. "Which of these thingamabobs means 'go'?"

Hodge rolled his eyes and sighed. If he didn't help her, she'd start hitting buttons until one of them did something, and he hadn't survived three Hags just to be killed in a machine mishap.

He pointed to the middle lever. "This lever controls direction. And this button says 'lift', which would be my bet on what's next."

Kane jammed the button down and the whirling turned to a grinding as the coils, aided by mechanics and enchantment, unrolled four spidery legs through the floor, lifting the house several feet in the air. The children huddled in a protective circle in the middle of the room, crying out as the house moved beneath them. Tilting first to the left, then swaying abruptly to the right, the house righted itself with a jerk. Hodge slid several feet across the room before catching himself on the cabinet and holding on to the knobs for dear life. The much more agile Kane leaned into each tilt, keeping her purchase at the helm.

After a few terrifying false starts, Hodge even going so far as to cross himself, Kane navigated the walking cottage through a rear loading door of the factory and into the street, minus only some thatching lost to a low-hanging rafter.

The house clunk-clanked through the streets, the panicked screams of residents and carriage horses announcing their path. One by one, Kane and Hodge returned the children to their homes in time for dinner. And, though they were delivered by an awkward mobile cottage instead of a red sleigh, there could be no better present than the safe return of their children in time for the morning Christmas celebrations. For Kane, it was seeing the smile and happy tears on Katie's face when her brother swept her up in his arms.

"What do you plan to do with this contraption?" Hodge asked once all the children had been returned.

"I rather like the idea of having a house I can take with me everywhere," Kane replied, now manipulating the gears with ease. "I think I'll keep it."

"Where!?"

Kane smiled, imagining his reaction when he realized where she meant to park it. "You let me worry about that, Hodges."

"Hodge!" he gritted through anxiety-clenched teeth, white knuckles gripping the counter as he watched pedestrians scramble below in terror. "And you're insufferable!"

"Pfft, you wouldn't have me any other way," she teased. "I'm the only thing keeping you from the brink of boredom and, secretly, you love our dangerous little escapades."

Hodge fumed but didn't reply. By the gods, but he hated it when she was right!

ABOUT THE AUTHOR

Fantasy author Sianyn Leigh grew up reading old fairy tales at her grandmother's knee, instilling in her a passion for history, mythology, and the importance of story-telling.

Obsessed with the rich pantheons, folklore, and superstitions across the world, she enjoys exploring the "what ifs" of life's many questions and weaving them into fanciful tales.

Infinitely more entertained by a rich fantasy life than reality, Sianyn has embarked upon a journey of sharing her musings with the world in the hopes others may also be entertained. She founded Chaos and Ink Books in early 2024 and hopes to provide tomes upon tomes of entertainment to readers for years to come.

Sianyn interned with a senior editor for two years assisting with clients and copywriting, and completed a writing course from the University of Queensland. She currently squeezes writing time and business operations around her day job in Medical Billing.

When not writing or working, you can find Sianyn binge-watching her favorite TV shows, entertaining two energetic dogs, and sleeping.

You can check her website at www.chaosinkbooks.com, where she posts event appearances, book updates, writing tips, and random mythology.